SAWDUST FIRES

A NOVEL

By Thomas E. Carlson

Published by T. Carlson
2440 Eighth Street
Muskegon Hts, MI 49444

This book is a work of fiction. The characters described are products of the author's imagination. Any resemblance to actual persons is entirely coincidental.

Copyright © 1998 by Thomas E. Carlson
All rights reserved

ISBN 0-9665487-0-1

Published by T. Carlson

Printed by Dobb Printing of Muskegon, Michigan

To my wife Kay

who has helped in so many ways

PREFACE AND ACKNOWLEDGMENTS

The writer of any historical novel must first decide how actual history will constrain the story. Some writers, such as Paul Maier, have written novels which come close to documentaries, adding only a few fictional characters to carry the narrative and then staying strictly within the facts. I'm not talented enough to produce such a novel. Moreover, I feel uneasy using real people in a fictional setting.

All this is to say the characters in this novel are entirely fictitious. Some of the historical events are described just as they happened. For instance, the death of Chief Sitting Bull occurred in December of 1890, just as in the story. But most events have been fictionalized, and the actions of the two main characters are complete fiction. The excerpts from the Muskegon Daily Chronicle are genuine and a listing of their appearances in the paper begins on page 185.

While reading portions of this story to my writing group I was continually asked to add sketches or photos. Either the listeners thought my descriptions so vapid as to need augmentation, or (as I prefer to believe) so vivid they excited a craving for even more detail. In any case I thought the inclusion of photos would make the book too much a documentary. Eventually I compromised by doing a separate pictorial. That companion booklet (*Muskegon - at the Peak of the Lumber Era*) should interest those seeking a more factual account of the times.

Thanks to the members of the writer's group, Poets and Prosers, for their encouragement. Thanks also go to the staffs of the Hackley Public Library and the Muskegon County Museum for their kind help and the use of their research facilities.

TOM CARLSON

LUMBER QUEEN

Twenty years ago old croakers said "Five or ten years more will exhaust the timber supply of Muskegon." They have said the same thing every year from that time to this until their prognostications are now considered about as reliable as those of the ordinary weather prophet.

> 1883 promotional booklet,
> declaring Muskegon "Lumber
> Queen of the World"

Ch 1

"I warned ye and now I order ye!" roared the boss riverman. "Get yerselves back up the bluff. Ye want logs flying down on yer pumpkin heads?"

"Go about your work, man," yelled back Petronius Frisk, good naturedly. "We'll do fine as spectators without your coaching." He heard a few nervous chuckles of agreement from the two dozen around him, mostly men plus a few boys and one woman.

Seeing the group not about to give way, the river boss turned with a low oath. Gingerly hopping from log to log he made his way back onto the river, taking time to swat at one of his crew whose face showed a smirk.

Petronius would have much preferred being out on the river rather than just a spectator. The battle impressed him as nothing less than a great sporting contest.

So it must have seemed also to the thousand or so gathered up on the bluff, brought from town by newspaper headlines such as: "Biggest Log Jam in Three Decades -- Over 100 Million Feet of Logs Upstream -- Rivermen in Constant Danger -- Dynamite May be Needed!"

Some had camped on the bluff with tents, bringing their wives and children. Others had come just for the day, putting down canvas ground covers and blankets against the March chill.

A few privileged families had provided themselves all the amenities of town, carting out chairs and folding tables. For them, servants laid down silver and china on white linen and drew repasts from large hampers.

Quite a large number of carriages and wagons were scattered all about the bluff, with their horses let loose to graze or to just wait patiently in harness.

The flood of logs filling the river had at first reminded Petronius of a giant glacier, or rather a picture he had seen of a glacier. Not the same material of course but similar pressures. Logs, some huge, had been lifted and posed at every angle, even straight up. Little gushers proved the pent up force of the river. Along with the rush of water came a straining sound which those nearest the river could feel through their skins. It was as if many ropes were being twisted tighter and tighter, and getting quite near their breaking points.

The log drivers now appeared to have all their dynamite charges in place and they hustled to either bank. The man with the plunger yelled, "Connecting the wires!"

Those on the bluff pressed close to the edge and jockeyed for the best viewing spots. Without any further warning a blast of water shot 100 feet into the air from all across the river, carry six dozen logs end over end. Amidst sprays of bark and foam a couple of the logs thudded down on shore, but well clear of Petronius and his group.

The jam-up of logs shuddered, appeared to move, then hesitated. The boss river driver ordered his men out with their poles and peaveys. They frantically began pulling logs loose on the downriver side. The mass shook again and one of the loggers fell and disappeared except for a foot sticking up. The spill went unnoticed by others in the crew. Those on shore yelled a warning but couldn't be heard above the tumult.

Petronius tossed his hat onto the sand and scrambled out towards the injured man. The bark on the logs looked rough but proved surprisingly slippery. After only 20 feet he lost his balance and went over sidewise. For a moment he felt himself wedged down, he face submerged in cold water. Fighting off panic, he twisted his body about and pulled himself up onto a log with his good arm. Instinctively he looked towards shore and saw the woman coming towards him.

"Just hold on!" she yelled and passed by.

Pulling himself higher, Petronius watched her progress, skitter-stepping from log to log. At times her high laced shoes lost their grip, but she recovered and danced on until she reached the stunned logger. Using the man's pole she pried him upwards. By then another logger had noticed the activity and gotten over. Together they hoisted and wrestled the injured man towards shore, and after many slips and near tumbles reached the safety of the river bank.

Petronius also got himself to shore, though clumsily, like a drunken crab. As he stumbled onto the sand he saw the people on the bluff clapping, though the sounds of the river reduced the action to pantomime. He knew the applause wasn't for him and could only hope people didn't think him too much a fool.

Petronius was offered a blanket as he retook his spot among the watchers. At first he refused, but after shivering for several minutes in his wet clothes he sought out the covering and wrapped it around himself.

The focus quickly changed back to the river. The jam was beginning to break and move, not with the great speed of a cattle stampede which Petronius had expected, but fast enough. It flowed with grinding and drumming noises, accompanied by booms and splashes as logs somersaulted their way back into the water and downstream.

More boys had come down from the bluff and were running along the shore, keeping progress with the moving crest. One of the river drivers, seeing an eager audience, jumped into a big log which had floated free. He spun the log with his feet fast enough to send up a spray of water, then jumped it to a stop and reversed the rotation.

The group around Petronius began to drift away. He returned the borrowed blanket and approached the woman who had performed the rescue. He would have preferred to slink away but it would be cowardly not to acknowledge her deed.

She was young, in her early 20's, and stood exceptionally tall, an inch or two higher than himself. Under her cloak she wore a plain white shirtwaist with long black skirt still dripping wet at the bottom. Her features looked somewhat mis-formed, as if her face had been made of wax and at some point had gotten to close to a flame, causing the skin to melt and droop.

"Along with everyone else I wish to add my compliments," he said. "Remarkable thing for a woman to do."

She laughed. I've done many of the things men have done."

He felt a bit of rebuke in her answer. "I meant to say you acted as bravely as anyone could, man or woman."

She accepted his apology. "You acted bravely also." She spoke with a young girlish voice, but with a lot of confidence behind it.

"Foolish I was," he said. "Old instincts took over."

"Your very best instincts I should think."

He had to admit to himself it wasn't so much his instinct to save a life as to show off his athleticism and be admired for it.

She noticed his twisted arm and asked, "Did you hurt yourself on the logs?"

"This is from a previous accident. Just got wet clothes this time." As he touched his hat and made a move to go she extended her hand.

"My name is Adelaide Driscoll."

Sawdust Fires 5

He gave his name as Larson, Jacob Larson, and shook her hand with his own left.

"Are you staying in town?"

"Occidental Hotel."

"Have you a ride back?"

"I've got a rented horse."

"That won't be very comfortable. I'm thinking of your wet clothes in this wind. My carriage has side curtains and you could tie your horse behind."

"Most kind, but I don't need to trouble you."

"It would be no trouble. We'll first need to collect my sketch pad from the edge of the bluff and then find my horse."

"An artist are you?" he asked as they began picking their way up the steep slope, at times on all fours.

"Oh, no. I draw and do some water coloring but I've had no training. I only wish I had the talent to really capture such events as this." She turned her head toward him. "And what is your business, Mr. Larson?"

"I'm a land buyer."

"Not timberland I hope? That's about gone."

"Cutover land, for farming."

"There's plenty of that everywhere in the State. Whether any of it is worth farming I don't know. My father is a lumberman. If you'd care to stop at his office he'll offer you as much cutover land as you'll ever want."

"I may do that," he said, without a lot of conviction.

The crowd was already beginning to disperse at the top of the bluff. Families were busily loading wagons and harnessing horses and mules for departure. The wind blew colder.

They retrieved Miss Driscoll's sketch pad and a folder of completed drawings.

"Let's see the one you made today," he said.

"With a look of chagrin she flipped back through some minor sketches to reveal her main rendering of the log jam. "I'm ashamed at what poor work I do," she said.

"It does look a little cock-eyed in spots," he agreed.

"Still, I want to record as much as I can. I'm sure our wonderful lumber business has seen its best days, and perhaps our town as well. It makes me sad."

"I see a lot of construction in town," he objected. "New street railroad going in too."

"Most people don't realize how quickly the timber is running out. The lumbermen do."

They rounded up the Driscoll horse and harnessed it to her carriage.

He was having seconds thoughts about riding with her. She seemed like a nosey burgher, and, after his embarrassing display on the river, he preferred to be alone.

"I believe I'll just ride by myself back to town," he said.

She gave him a scolding look but couldn't talk him out of it.

"At least take my blanket to keep warm," she said

"I'll take your blanket, Miss, and with thanks."

Just before driving off she asked, "Are you from the East?"

"No. Chicago."

"Ah, Chicago." She gave a derisive little laugh. "Then you need no advice from me." She made her voice more cordial. "Still, Mr. Larson, if either I or my father can be of help, please call on us."

Petronius accepted the jibe without anger. Frankly he agreed with her. It was a thing of pride to be from Chicago. And he didn't need the advice of Muskegonites.

He looked for his own horse in some haste. He could see the sky dark and threatening to the west. The wind grew stronger and soon snow flakes swirled thickly about him.

He rode quickly at first but then slowed the horse as the unfamiliar trail grew harder to see. Gusts of wind made it difficult to hold the blanket around himself as he rode. He cursed the weakness in his right arm.

At one point the covering came completely loose from his grasp and he had to jump off the horse and chase after it. The grey blanket flew like a kite before the wind until, after a hundred yards, it wrapped itself about a tree.

As Petronius remounted his horse he was ready to concede he'd made a mistake in not accepting the carriage ride.

PROMISING OUTLOOK

Muskegon has now a wide reputation for energy, enterprise, hospitable and wide awake people, and for keeping steadily in the van of those Michigan cities noted for rapid and substantial growth and progress, based upon exceptional natural advantages of climate and location, with capital, energy, and modern ideas of their use to utilize these and make the most of them. No city of it's size today has a more promising outlook for future development and continued success.

1889 Muskegon City Directory

Ch 2

After two days of coughing, nose blowing and other assorted miseries, Petronius emerged from his bed in the Occidental Hotel. He hadn't left the room even for meals, having hot soup sent up.

He bathed his face and upper body with steaming hot towels, feeling thankful he hadn't come down with pneumonia. While putting on a shirt, always a struggle with his bad arm, he looked again at the note sent up from the lobby. "Mr. Jacob Larson, we have <u>important</u> information for you." A time and place were named. The invitation had all the makings of a rouse and a setup, but he would go anyway, glad to have an excuse to be doing something.

After shaving he put on his rough suit. He wouldn't have to maintain the look of a prosperous businessman for this meeting. He dispensed with perfumey lotion but slicked down his short dark hair before putting his bowler hat firmly in place. His illness had given him a bit of a pallor, yet his demeanor mostly satisfied him. It was a lean face, with enough of a hawk nose to give him the appearance of an ascetic. His eyes, though, lacked the proper intense and purposeful look. He regretted that, and at times practiced a squint to look menacing.

Before leaving the room he looked about to fasten in his mind how his things were placed. The room had been searched before. Nothing could be found of course. What letters he had resided in a bank deposit box, along with his revolver.

In the lobby he asked the desk clerk for the past Daily Chronicles, wanting to catch any news missed during his sick time. Nothing arrested his eye except the newspaper account of the log jam. Young Miss Driscoll's part in the rescue of the riverman came in for some praise, but not without reservation. Part of the story, written in a bantering fashion, implied she was a bit of a gadabout, though of good character, and placed herself too much in the situations of men, though handling them well enough.

The air outside the hotel gave some promise of Spring. Even the breeze felt warm, though the day was approaching evening. Petronius looked up at the hotel's three levels of verandas, with their balustrades all streaked with soot. He could see some of the culprit smokestacks a short distance away, sending out the acrid odor of wood burning steam boilers.

He walked east on Western Avenue, a street which looked as if it were becoming the main business thoroughfare. No carriages or other traffic plied it now because the track for a street railway was being laid down its middle. A sign with colorful bunting announced the project with phrases like, "the continued upward progress of our forward looking city, etc, etc."

Petronius stepped around another pile of sand, this from the beginnings of a large basement. A surprising amount of construction was going on to be sure. Old wooden buildings with their false fronts and tar paper roofs were being replaced by solid brick structures of two and three stories. Solid, but of questionable architecture. Might take some lessons from our Chicago builders, he thought. When he reached the opera house he paused to gaze up at a half dozen Turkish style turrets piled atop fancy roof parapets. He commented to another pedestrian, "Fella who designed that should have stuck to making circus wagons!"

As he passed a store window he caught his reflection. Arm makes me look like a fool cripple, he thought. He recalled how he used to walk, arms outstretched, a picture of considerable grace and strength. Now he felt out of balance swinging just one arm.

After four more blocks the street began to slope down. He was headed for an area referred to as "the sawdust flats," along the rim of the lake and towards the mouth of the river. Originally it had been marsh land, then a dumping area for sawdust and bark scraps. After a time the waste material built up deep and hard enough for foundations of buildings as well as streets and sidewalks.

Most of the town's saloons congregated down in the flats. On an earlier tour he had counted almost four dozen. Clumps of three and four stood side by side, with an occasional harness store, restaurant, or tailor shop breaking the monopoly.

Often the taverns were grouped by nationality. There was Doyle's, Fitzgerald's and Flynn's for the Irish. The Germans could look to Bosch's and Meier's and Pfenning's. Scandinavian imbibers had Hollstrom's or Nystrom's or Finlayson's. For the French, the Gagnon, the Peltier, and the Vasseur were offered. Many tried for colorful titles, with red being most used. He had noticed the Red Deer, the Red Keg and the Red Sash.

The place he looked for, the Big Deal saloon, resided at the rag-tail end of Ottawa Street, in a narrow building of unpainted vertical siding. Several rooms upstairs probably served as a brothel. The door stood open to let in the less tarnished outside air. Splintered wood around the hinges suggested the door might not close properly anyway. Though he didn't feel totally fit for service he decided to plunge in.

Kerosene lamps provided some lighting but cigar smoke made it look as though there was a fog in the main bar room. A faded woodcut on one wall pictured something with Greek or Roman columns. The bar itself had an impromptu look, as if constructed of discarded lumber. Pock marks peppered the top, evidently from loggers walking on it with their calked boots.

Petronius counted 14 men in the place, some together at tables. A woman, looking old enough to be a great grandmother, sat at the end of the bar reading a book. Petronius ordered a liverwurst sandwich with a beer and sat at one of the tables. When the food came he had to force it down, though liverwurst was usually one of his favorites. He hoped the bad taste was due to his sore throat.

After he had eaten he got up and handed a note to the old lady. As he moved away he caught the title of her book, "Treasure Island." When Petronius had resumed his seat the woman made an eye signal to a couple of men at the bar. They came to the table, bringing an aroma of strong drink.

The bigger of the two had a grizzled red beard. As he sat down he offered his hand across the table. "Louie Pattone, at your service he is sure." He waved a hand towards the other man. "Shelvay, he is my friend."

The smaller fellow had eyes which sloped down, giving him an expression of benign sadness. A brimmed hat perched on the back of his head.

"Jacob Larson," said Petronius, "as you already know. Shall we get right to our business?"

"Whiskey here!" bellowed Pattone over his shoulder. "The new man will pay."

"Cancel that," Petronius called sharply to the bartender. "Gentlemen, I'll buy a glass of beer, nothing more."

"Beer," scoffed Pattone. "No woodsman will drink beer."

"I'm a businessman, so it's beer at my table. Now what's your information?"

"My friend, Shelvay, he would like to know, how much do you pay us for our secrets?"

"I'll decide after I've heard your information. Won't promise anything ahead of time."

Pattone's voice took on a more refined tone. "As you say. Then let us get to be friends a little first. Your business here, tell some more of it so we know better how to, how shall I say, cooperate with your needs."

"Don't have much to say myself. My need is to hear why you brought me down here to this rat hole."

Pattone forced a smile and waved his hand about. "This saloon, she is a good place for talk. Shelvay and I will tell you some little of ourselves and then perhaps you will share your own stories with us."

Petronius put on his hat and sneered. "Not a very clever pair of fishermen are you?"

Pattone grabbed across the table but Petronius brushed the hand away and jumped to his feet. The big man knocked the table to one side. Men at other tables moved quickly to a side of the room. Pattone swung a huge fist which Petronius easily avoided. Three more punches struck only air, but Petronius felt his coat tear at the shoulder as he twisted away from one.

Shelvay, standing to one side, called out, "Not usually is he a violent man."

Petronius dodged two more blows.

"Quite gentle he is, when he has not been drinking."

A mallet which Pattone threw from the bar glanced off Petronius' right arm.

"Tomorrow he will be your friend. Tomorrow he will say he is sorry." Shelvay's face showed a certain urgency, as if wanting Petronius to concede the point. At the same time he seemed to be edging around behind, as if looking for an opening.

Sawdust Fires   13

Pattone lowered his head and rushed, bull-like. Petronius pirouetted to one side and yelled to Shelvay. "Out of the way, man! Unless you can get an apology now!"

Shelvay stood with a hurt look on his face for a few seconds before moving off to the side of the room.

Pattone again charged, this time aiming for the groin. Petronius slapped hard at the man's ear. As Pattone wheeled about, Petronius slapped the same ear, and again, until it bulged red. Pattone roared, grabbed a chair and flung it. Petronius evaded most of it but one leg caught him above the eye. He heard a ringing in his ears. As Pattone charged again, Petronius dropped down and swung the chair so an edge caught the bearded man just below the knee.

While Pattone went down on all fours in pain, Petronius retrieved his hat and made towards the door, wobbling a little sideways as he walked. He noticed the old woman still engrossed in her book.

Back at his hotel room Petronius saw an unsigned note which had been slipped under the door. It read, "We know all about you and what you are doing here." The note rather troubled him. But his head hurt too much to think much about it. He took a triple dose of his cough medicine and headed for bed, thinking maybe he did need some advice.

TERRIBLE LOSS

The Michigan Shingle and Lumber Company mill burned to the ground last night; the fire starting in some unknown manner between 3AM and 4AM. Two night watchmen, apparently busy in the boiler room, gave no signal. Firemen at the Number 6 Hose Company, nearly a mile away, saw the blaze and sounded the alarm.

Muskegon Daily Chronicle

Ch 3

Most of the pine trees had been dispensed with Petronius noted as he walked in one of the fashionable areas of town. The trees left standing were mostly oaks and maples. Of course leafy trees furnished better shade in the summer but their bare branches did little now to block any of the late morning sun. But the sun was welcome on this crisp day.

The Driscoll house resided on a large plat of land in the shape of an oval, along with seven other well spaced mansions. All were constructed of ornate wood. That was a mistake, he thought. Wealthy families in Chicago had learned their lesson from the great fire of 1871, and now built their palaces of stone and brick.

He felt much refreshed from a good sleep though the hoarseness in his voice lingered. Settling on some course of action had also buoyed his spirits. He took the pleasant stroll completely around the oval, admiring the houses. Multiple chimneys stretched high amidst the peaks and gables of the roofs. Ornamental iron work graced many of the roofs, sometimes in the form of decorative fencing, other times topping off a turret with a slender weather vane or Neptune's trident.

The center of the oval had been left open, like a park,

with thick bushes, some medium sized trees and a few gardens, though nothing very orderly. He noted too, a sort of gazebo made of weathered timber and having a high little cupola with climbing ladder.

The Driscoll home wasn't the largest but, to Petronius, one of the more inviting because of its many porches and balconies. As he made his way up a front walk composed of octagon shaped wooden blocks, he noted paint flaking off the fancy scroll work of the house and calking loose around windows.

His knock was answered by a dour faced house keeper. "Addy got yer message and is expectin' you," she growled as she led him to a sitting room made bright and airy by its high ceiling and many windows.

Miss Driscoll perched rather gracefully on a stool, a grey cat nestled in her lap. She was adding water coloring to one of her sketches.

Petronius handed over a well laundered and folded blanket with appropriate thanks. "Also brought you some candy, in gratitude," he said, presenting a prettily wrapped box.

"Oh, how thoughtful."

"No trouble. Candy shop is right next to the hotel." He felt gratitude also for Miss Driscoll's misformed face. Around beautiful women he tried overly much to joke and be clever. Not that he associated with many beautiful women.

She offered him a chair and a look of sympathy as the raspiness of his voice. "I'm sorry the blanket didn't prevent your catching a cold. Is that bruise in any way related?"

He touched the purplish bump on his forehead.

"This is from a business meeting. Turned out badly."

"Land buying must be more contentious than I thought," she said

"This man, Louie Pattone, who is he?"

"Louie Pattone? I don't recognize the name. Sounds French. Is he a businessman?"

"Woodsman, he said."

"Lots of Quebecers work in the logging camps and in the mills. What business did you have with Mr. Pattone?"

"Said he had useful information. I believe he was sent to find out things about me. Or scare me off." He related some of the incident.

She gave me a reassuring look. "Perhaps just a cruel prank. In our town the lumbermen and loggers can be provincial towards outsiders. Their first reaction is to bully. Some will start a fight just for the love of fighting. It's part of their manhood." Her tone and formal use of words reminded him of a teacher.

"I put a more sinister face on things, Miss."

"Sinister? In what way?"

"I see people following me and watching me in strange ways."

"Then you should go to the police."

"Wouldn't work. Some of those watching have been policemen."

She gave him a more questioning look.

He tried to explain. "I've been a policeman myself, and a detective."

"You were once a policeman and now you're a land speculator?"

"Truth is I'm a detective hired by the insurance companies to investigate the sawmill fires."

She let out a surprised breath. "You go too fast for me, Mr. Larson. Start again."

He got to his feet and folded his bad arm behind his back as if ready to give a speech. "Better than a week ago I arrived by train, presenting myself as a land buyer. A mistake maybe, but I thought it'd give me time to look things over and talk openly to people. Not so. From the start I got suspicious looks and guarded answers."

"Understandable if they somehow knew you were an insurance investigator."

He showed her the note slipped under his door. "They say they know who I am and what I'm doing. But I don't believe it. Yesterday morning while I ate breakfast a man tried to make a quick sketch of me. For identification purposes I'd say."

She shook her head. "I admit I'm puzzled. Also I'm not clear about the note you sent to me."

"I'm floundering, Miss. Like a fish on the pier. I need help. I recalled your offer."

"My offer was in the way of business help, land buying and such."

He raised a finger. "Let me ask you this. What sort of newcomer would get the kind of scrutiny I've had?"

She thought for several seconds. "A union organizer perhaps."

"I don't think I've acted like a union organizer. That bears some thought though. Any other ideas?"

She shook her head. After a minute's silence she said, "My suggestion is to announce yourself as an investigator and make clear how you intend to go about your business."

"I see. Tell all, then see how things develop. Makes sense. Probably the best course." he resumed his seat. "But I'm a stubborn man and want to see how this plays out. Now then, I'd like to hire your services."

"In what way?"

"I need to learn about this lumber business and your town of Muskegon. I'll pay reasonable for your time. Starting this minute if it's no trouble."

She gave a little laugh and began to say something, but could only get a word out before laughing again. Perhaps she was thinking of their earlier conversation after the log jam.

Sawdust Fires 18

When she had got control of herself she said, "I don't mean to laugh but you are surprising. What do you want to do?"

"You decide."

"We can tour my father's mill if you like. I'll get my hat and cloak. But I've not yet agreed to your offer, Mr. Larson. I won't give my answer until I've had time to consider."

As they walked briskly towards the lake front Petronius took a second to admire Miss Driscoll's long graceful stride. At the same time he gave her bad marks for her tall, skinny figure. Certainly nothing close to the renowned Gibson girl.

"That labor trouble," he began. "How did it play out?"

"The mill workers struck over working hours. 'Ten hours or no sawdust,' so the slogan went."

"How many hours was the normal working day?"

"Eleven or twelve, depending on the mill. And often six days a week when lumber orders were pressing."

"The lumbermen won out did they?"

"Yes. But for a time it appeared the mill hands would get their ten hours. A lot of the community backed them. Their arguments made sense. Most mill accidents occur when the men are tired at the end of long days. Certainly accidents cost the mill owners money too."

"So what happened?"

"The lumbermen brought in hundreds of replacement workers from Canada. The lumber market was soft and some mills just shut down for eight weeks. You can imagine the desperation of families without income for so long. So the demands were dropped. Strangely enough some years after that a state law ordered a ten hour work day."

"Any fighting during the strike?"

"I seem to recall one mill partly burned and several people beaten on both sides. Pinkerton detectives were brought in. For a time men walked about with rifles and shotguns. But the war many predicted never happened."

"Was the strike organized by outsiders mostly?"

"I don't remember. But no, I think the main advocates were local men."

"Your father, which way did he go?"

She made a wry face. "He said he would agree with the ten hours but he couldn't do it on his own. And bucking the big men would bring the worst kind of trouble."

"Ain't that so!" Petronius said with some enthusiasm.

She looked over in question.

"I've had some experience bucking big men." He offered no further details.

The lake came into view and with it several lumber mills. They headed for a green building consisting of a large shed with several minor sheds attached, one of which supported two large smoke stacks. Neat vertical siding and well placed windows gave the structure an almost domestic look, although a coat of fresh paint was needed. A narrow platform atop the peak of the roof supported two dozen water barrels as a guard against fire.

"Have you ever visited, a sawmill, Mr. Larson?"

"Can't say I have."

"My friends and I grew up playing in sawmills, just as farm children grow up playing in barns."

"No more dangerous I expect."

They went around to the water side of the building. Docks and pilings extended well out into the lake, forming a giant enclosure for the floating timber. A half dozen men with long poles stood easily atop their logs, guiding them as if piloting gondolas. A trough ran from the water high up into the building. Men on either side drew the logs in with hooked poles until they caught on a continuous chain which clattered up the center of the trough.

"The heavy machinery fills most of the ground floor," she said, "so the logs are sent up to the upper level, which is the cutting floor. Oh, look here's a big one coming." She pointed to a log about four feet in diameter. "Let's watch it come into the head saw. Quickly."

They ran up a tramway, entered a side door and edged along the wall until they came in view of the opening where the logs entered. Floating sawdust clouded the air and the odor of pine resin mixed with the hot smell of saw blades and steam driven hardware. All the men in the building wore hats, mostly straight brimmed but a few derbies and a few slouch type. All were covered with a fine snow of sawdust.

The big log heaved its way in and settled into a groove, shaking the floor. Immediately a mechanism kicked the log sideways down a slight incline and it rolled against a pair of arms with sharp gripping fingers. Responding to hand signals from one man, two others of the crew adjusted the arms until the log was jogged into exact position. With the sound of steam piston being activated, the whole works slid forward into a bandsaw which sliced off a foot thick slab with considerable speed. As soon as the cut was made the carriage rolled back and the men reset the log for a second slice.

Petronius watched the first slab as it was pulled along some rollers and fed into another type of saw with twenty or more blades rocking up and down, cutting the slab into a like number of inch thick boards. Amazing, he thought, that a log so dark and rough on its outside could produce boards of such brightness, like a slice of fresh bread.

He felt the floor shake again as the log was turned onto its flat side. The lead man gave more signals and a different thickness cut was made.

The high whine and rip of the saws shut off talk so Petronius followed Miss Driscoll's lead. They walked up some steps onto a narrow catwalk from which most of the cutting floor could be seen, and then up a ladder for a brief look from a deck onto the roof. From there they went all the way down to the ground level, which was crowded with steam cylinders, large shafts, pulley belts and occasional carts for the bark edgings and sawdust which dropped from the cutting floor above.

Petronius could see the attraction for children; noise, dust, activity and lots of places to hide and climb. From the interested look on Miss Driscoll's face he could tell she kept her childish view of the place.

After a quick peek into an area where giant saw blades were being sharpened, they went into the boiler room. Miss Driscoll pulled a rope, setting off a shrill steam whistle. She laughed and they hurried out of the building just as a man came running, shaking his finger in admonition.

As they walked between piles of gleaming boards stacked criss-cross 20 feet high, Miss Driscoll explained she was due at her father's office to do book keeping and typewriting. But she would send Petronius a note when she had decided on his offer.

He wasn't sure why so much time was needed to decide. It seemed like a simple enough proposal.

DON'TS FOR GOOD GIRLS

Don't allow yourself to be under obligations to any man. Don't offer to shake hands when a man is introduced to you. Don't write, except when it can't be avoided, to men. Don't feel it necessary to bow to a man you have met at a ball or party afterwards, unless you want to continue the acquaintance.

Muskegon Daily Chronicle

Ch 4

The men who worked at the log sorting grounds called themselves "boomers," not because their activity caused loud noises but because their main tool of trade was the "boom," a floating fence for enclosing logs. Petronius had just read that explanation in the paper, though not in an article about lumbering. The story told of a plan to organize a professional ball team in Muskegon. Such team to play in a league with other Michigan cities like Grand Rapids and Lansing. Such team to play their games in a park on the north side of the lake. And such team to be nicknamed "The Boomers."

Indeed the baseball story was the second time he had read of boomers in two days. The first was at the library going through old Muskegon Daily Chronicles in search of details about the labor troubles eight years earlier. He had found the articles and the story had been pretty much as Miss Driscoll had described it, although the strike hadn't been started by the mill workers, but by the boomers. The mill hands, encouraged by the strike's early success, had joined the boomers later. Whether that difference had an importance he didn't know.

The next morning Petronius was anxious to get busy with useful work, but with so much boomer knowledge in hand he couldn't very well do anything but view the boomers in action. He would make it a working trip as well, taking along his

Sawdust Fires 23

pistol and doing some target practice further along the river. He needed experience using his left hand.

After retrieving his revolver from the bank deposit box he headed towards the Sawdust Flats and the mouth of the river.

The river flowed into the lake in three branches, with the branch closest to town being the main channel and also the log sorting area. A double row of a hundred or more pens occupied a good half mile of this waterway. The bridge for wagon and foot traffic made an excellent viewing spot and a couple dozen spectators already lounged along its railings. They were mostly old retired gents, but also a few boys who should have been in school.

The log pens weren't situated along the banks but anchored on pilings pretty much in the center of the river, with only a 30 foot wide log channel down the middle. Two or three men attended each pen, moving about on narrow walkways as they pulled the logs in with their long pikes.

The work was surely one of the less dramatic of the lumbering jobs, if not outright drudgery. A day on your feet, balancing on board pathways, some less than a foot wide, all the while hefting an awkward pole. Yet there was something attractive about the activity and even soothing. The logs flowed serenely down the central channel, making only the slightest clunking sounds, while the men bantered back and forth in cheerful voices as they went about their work. The boomers, about 300 of them, plied their poles with a smooth and efficient rhythm, reaching, pulling, poking, and acting like patient shepherds herding sheep. Most wore wide brimmed hats, as protection against the sun normally, though this day against the light rain falling.

Petronius tried to dope out the logic and plan of the sorting pens. No doubt there were several pens set aside for each mill, probably at regular intervals. That way if a log was missed by one station it would be pulled in later by another. Also, he surmised, the pens were set well out into the middle of the river to leave enough waterway to float the collected logs out the back of each pen.

While he watched, a full pen of logs, lined up orderly fashion, side by side and end to end, like a raft, was fastened together with lengths of chain and metal staples. A floating boom at the back of the pen was opened and the raft eased out until the river current caught it and moved it downstream. Petronius was told a large sea wall along the shore of the lake held the rafts of logs until tugboats could tow them, several dozen at a time, to their designated mills.

During a lull in the flow of logs, one of the boomers reached out with the end of his pole and nudged another man enough to send him, arms aflutter, splashing into the river. The school boys on the bridge laughed hysterically and then ran off, as if that was the only reason they had come. The dunked man, a young fellow, climbed out sputtering and wanting to fight. But the yell of a supervisor restored order. The fellow's hat was fished out of the water further downstream and passed back pole by pole.

Petronius began walking along a foot path upriver, intending to do his target practice against a bluff in that direction. But it was raining harder by then and he started to have second thoughts. The rain wasn't cold but it was coming down steady. His pistol was a new one, and he hesitated to expose it to water and possible rust. He turned back and decided he would visit the new ballpark in North Muskegon instead. He had an interest in ballparks and baseball, being a former player himself. In fact before his arm had been damaged he'd had the talent to play professional ball.

As he returned on the path he passed an old gent who had been with him on the bridge and the two nodded. As he walked further along Petronius glanced back. The old gent had also changed direction and was now following him. Petronius felt fairly certain the man had been assigned to keep a watch on his activities.

Sawdust Fires 25

The north side of the lake seemed a poor choice for the ballpark. First of all the branches of the river had to be crossed. The wooden bridges appeared adequate but nothing to inspire over-confidence. When he crossed the third bridge he had to stop and brace his legs as a freight wagon clattered over, setting off vibrations and swaying. The road connecting the bridges and traversing the rest of the marsh was a rough affair as well, constructed mostly of logs set crosswise in the swampy ground with a topping of planks along the line of travel.

When Petronius reached the high ground on the north side of the lake he had to trudge another mile to reach the village of North Muskegon. There he was told the ballpark was yet another two miles further along the shore of the lake. A wooden walkway had been provided at least and the path proved scenic. Much of the forest, mixed pines and hardwoods, had been left in place, even though a dozen sawmills operated on the north side of the lake. Looking over the lake he could see the clear outlines of the sawmills and business buildings directly across, but those to either end of the lake faded out in mist and smoke. He could hear the muted sounds of industry, the banging of pile drivers, the chug of tugboats hauling logs and the constant buzz of saws and cutting. But in spite of all the activity the whole town of Muskegon had a country feel and look to it, at least in comparison to Chicago.

The ballpark rested on a bluff amid a grove of tall pines. A name board proclaimed "Interlake Park." A charming locale, he thought. However the small covered grandstand disappointed him. Constructed of rough lumber and adequate for 500 or 600 spectators, it lacked any real decoration or even pleasing proportions. A coat of white paint did add a little dignity. The field itself had been graded well enough, but the grass, starting to show green under the Spring rains, grew in irregular tufts.

Petronius sat in the grandstand, resting out of the rain. He noticed the old gent following him had settled against a tree some distance away, his collar turned up against the rain while he lighted a pipe.

Petronius rested a while longer and then got up and walked directly towards the old fellow. At first the man looked startled when he realized Petronius was approaching, but then relaxed and made as if his pipe totally absorbed him.

"Why are you watching me, man?" said Petronius when he got close. "And who are you working for?"

"I warn't doing none of that sir, no," he replied in an apologetic and almost surprised voice.

"You were, and I want to know about it." Petronius hooked a toe back of the man's boot and shoved him to the wet ground. The pipe scattered sparks as it tumbled away.

"No sir, I warn't," the man repeated several times as he held up a hand to shield his face.

Petronius cuffed him on the side of the head. If he inflicted enough pain he could make the beggar talk. He brought out his pistol and was prepared to stick it in the man's eye and draw back the hammer. He saw the hurt and fear in the man's face and couldn't bring himself to go any further. He turned and walked back towards the village, feeling angry at himself for not being harder, more resolute.

At the village he hired a ride back to town and his hotel. He changed to dry clothes and stopped at the hotel's main desk before going into the dining room for a late lunch. A note, sealed with wax, had been left in his box. It proved to be from Miss Driscoll.

"I've considered your proposal to hire my time," it read. "Your investigation of the mill fires interests me. Especially since it involves one of the McClatchen mills. Also, I would welcome some income to finance my various little projects. However, I will enter your employ only under certain conditions. First, you must be entirely open with me in all particulars, both as to your investigation and your background. Second, I expect you to give some weight to my advice when it is offered.

"This is not to demand an equal partnership in your undertakings. I realize I haven't your experience. But I do have some intelligence and a wish to be more than a hireling. My father employs me in many of his business tasks but doesn't confide in me with regard to important matters. This causes me anguish and I have no wish to involve myself in another such situation.

"Excuse this rambling and rather emotional letter. As you can tell I've had some difficulty getting my thoughts on paper. If you accept my terms please advise immediately by note. Also, you are invited to dinner by my father this evening at seven regardless of your answer. I've told him you are a land buyer and possibly interested in some of his cutover timberland." The note was signed Adelaide (Addy) Driscoll.

Rather a strange letter, Petronius thought. Still he didn't ponder too long before sending his reply. "Terms agreed to," it said, "as long as I'm not expected to heal over the gaps between you and your father."

He spent the rest of the afternoon relaxing and reading sports in the Police Gazette.

EVOLUTION EXPLAINED
Professor Geddes calls attention to two tendencies in organic evolution -- the vegetative and the reproductive -- and asserts that evolution is the result of the universal subordination of the former to the latter.

Muskegon Daily Chronicle

Ch 5

Petronius arrived at the Driscoll house looking very much the earnest business man in pressed suit and starched collar. Addy greeted him at the door and suggested they talk briefly in the garden area before going in to meet her father.

"We call this area our common, because it's shared by all the houses." She directed him towards a bench near the gazebo like structure. "It's always been more of a play area for children than a place for planting gardens."

"I envy you growing up in these surroundings," he said.

"What were your circumstances?"

"I was raised in an orphanage."

They sat down. The lowering sun cast a long shadow from one of the houses, almost reaching their feet.

"I can sympathize with that," she said. "My own mother died when I was just four." She paused and scrunched up her face. "I shouldn't have said that. I certainly couldn't call myself an orphan. I've lived a privileged life here. In fact I had a lovely childhood. The other houses had several girls of my age and we became wonderful companions. The pond over there was our ocean and the gazebo our pirate ship. Our mountain was that pine tree and those lilac bushes a jungle, and we would run and sail and fly. Summer nights when we were supposed to be asleep we would signal each other from upstairs balconies with candles." She stopped in some embarrassment. "I'm sorry."

"No need to apologize. I was given a fair upbringing and a fair education at St. Ignatius. Spent a year at the seminary in fact."

She looked more at ease. "Well, let's talk about the business ahead. Do you feel you can hold your own if my father discusses the particulars of land buying?"

"I think I can bluff my way through."

"If you feel stumped, change the subject to social philosophy. That interests him greatly these days and he can talk at length. Shall we go in?" She got up and led the way towards the house.

The few windows in the dining room of the mansion faced east and were shaded from the sun. Adding to the dark atmosphere were walls of walnut paneling. Gas lights along the wall added some brightness. Mr. Driscoll sat at the head of the table with Petronius and Addy placed on either side. The housekeeper brought out baked chicken with rice and vegetables. Petronius felt out of place in a fine house but he had been taught enough table manners at school to cope with social situations.

After they had finished the main course Mr. Driscoll began talking business. His tones came out Irish brogue but not overly strong. "Show him that land in Missaukee County, Addy. Those sections should be makin' fine farms. Not too hilly with some good lakes. And when you go up there you can update the survey on the Leota stand. This comes at a good time." He looked greatly pleased and turned to Petronius. "Mr. Larson, my daughter will be of great assistance to you. She knows more about lumberin' than most men."

"Oh, why do you say that father, when you don't think it?" Addy said in a hurt voice.

Her father gave a snorting laugh. He was a bulky man but carefully dressed. A very short beard covered much of his face, making him look dark and morose. He continued addressing Petronius. "Some have called us plunderers, but we lumbermen are furtherin' the progress of this region immensely by clearing the land for settlement and farming. And with farming will come more prosperity and cities too. Mr. Larson, have you been readin' any of the naturalist philosophers?"

"If they weren't serialized in Sporting Life then probably I haven't." When the joke went unnoticed he added, "Lately I have had time to read what you might call good literature. Cooper's 'Last of the Mohicans,' I've read just a few weeks ago."

Driscoll snorted again. "Suitable for diversion, but not for understandin' the rough and tumble of today's society." He spread out his hands. "All of nature, we find, is strivin'. Only not enough sunshine and water is there for every striver, so just the fittest live on. But because the hardiest and best survive, the planet progresses, is made richer, and all evolves to a higher state. We see it in the forests and we see it in human civilization. I greatly summarize and simplify, you understand."

"No doubt," said Petronius, his feelings hurt by having his choice of good literature panned. "But even your simplified form goes a bit beyond my capacities."

"Just so." Driscoll looked a bit uncomfortable, not sure he had been insulted or complimented. "Well, shall we let Addy and Mrs. Fogarty tidy up here while we're havin' our coffee in the library?"

While shifting rooms, Petronius was offered a cigar which he declined. Mr Driscoll placed himself in a large chair, folded one leg over the other and began puffing away. He eyed his cigar for a minute before addressing Petronius. "Mr. Larson, your interest in Addy is well placed. She is indeed a talented young lady and engages in much charitable work. As you've noticed her looks are, well, marred they are. She suffered from edema, a form of dropsy, while and infant.

You're to be commended for lookin' deeper than physical beauty. I myself was never one to put great stock in the outer beauty of a woman, though Addy's mother was a fine looking woman. Very fine looking indeed and much admired everywhere for her spirit and graciousness. Addy has many of the very---"

"Sir," Petronius interrupted. "You seem to have slid off the road a bit. I don't want to be ungrateful for dinner but I've got no romantic designs. I intend only a business arrangement with your daughter. Like you, I believe she knows a lot about the lumber business and can help me considerable."

"Ah, just so." Driscoll took a long draw on his cigar. His boot began to twitch. Finally he noticed it and forced it still. "Well," he said, "should you reconsider, keep in mind I shall be extendin' all financial help to Addy and whichever young man she decides upon. My wealth is diminished at present, but new prospects show themselves daily. Yes, daily."

"Most kind of you," Petronius responded.

They lapsed into silence. Addy came into the room finally and suggested she and Petronius take a short walk.

The night air was cool, but still pleasant enough for early Spring. They walked west to where the mansions of the wealthier lumbermen stood, each house with its barn and coach house occupying a fair piece of land, some almost an entire block. Lights showed in one of the houses but no people could be seen through the windows.

"I'm glad I didn't grow up in one of those places," said Addy. "They seem so isolated and without friends."

"Can't say I liked your father much," said Petronius.

She sighed. "He's been a troubled man the last few years."

"Financial difficulties?"

"Financial problems, yes, and this new philosophy which has hold of him, extolling survival of the fittest. Social Darwinism, some call it, after the naturalist Charles Darwin."

"Your father seems rather happy with it I'd say."

"But it gives him no comfort. And even contributes to his financial mistakes."

"How is that?"

"He's become obsessed with gaining social stature, to prove he's one of the fit, I suppose. With that in mind he entered into a timber deal with Mr. McClatchen about two years ago."

"Is that the same McClatchen whose sawmill just burned?"

"The same. McClatchen, as you probably know, is our most powerful lumberman. But my father didn't need McClatchen's financial backing because he held the purchase option himself. The whole thing was structured as a favor to McClatchen."

"Your father looked for a favor in return I expect?"

"McClatchen's backing him for membership in the Muskegon Club. The club had rejected his try for membership some years earlier."

"But with McClatchen on his side no one would object."

She nodded. "But it didn't work out."

They had reached the Driscoll house again and sat down in wicker chairs on the front porch. She continued her story. "They realized a profit of over $300,000 on the timberland, to be divided between them. Then for some reason McClatchen reneged. Either he did it as some monstrous joke or just to prove my father wasn't his equal in business. Or maybe it was simply greed."

"Explain to me," said Petronius, "how a fella makes $300,000 on a timber deal."

"It was land in Minnesota," she said. My father took out a purchase option almost 20 years ago. The land had excellent timber but without a river nearby to get the logs out. Then a few years ago a rail line went in and the timber became valuable. My father still needed to raise the cash to buy the land but that could have been done through a bank. Instead he went to McClatchen. They bought the land at the option price and immediately resold it to a Minnesota lumberman for three times the amount. But when it came time to split the money McClatchen stalled. He said no exact time had been agreed upon for settling accounts. My father went to court. McClatchen slipped away to Minneapolis and said urgent business kept him there. The court ordered McClatchen's bookkeeper to turn over the accounts, but before that could happen the bookkeeper was fired and the keys to McClatchen's safe spirited to Minneapolis. After more months of delay my father couldn't hold out any longer against his creditors and agreed to a much smaller amount, about $30,000 I believe."

"With no club membership thrown in?"

She laughed wryly. "I'm sure that membership has been a source of much scoffing and merriment at the Muskegon Club. And my father has been the butt of jokes outside the club as well, and that eats at him." She again sighed. "Another of my father's recent obsessions, as I'm sure you're aware, is to get me suitably married. He wants the Driscoll line to continue if not the Driscoll name."

"Wishes the best for you, I'm sure," Petronius replied lamely.

"I'm sure he does wish the best for me. He's been a generous father over the years and given me a fair degree of freedom. I only wish he'd take a little of my advice."

"Taking advice from women doesn't seem to come natural to men," he said.

She nodded in resignation.

They agreed on a time to meet the next morning when Petronius would tell his story.

UNUSUALLY FREE

Chicago's morgue accommodates fifty, and yet must be enlarged; a ghastly reminder of the shadowed side of life and death in a great city. Muskegon for its size is unusually free from the usual morgue horrors.

Muskegon Daily Chronicle

Ch 6

"Hard to know where to start," said Petronius. "Rather varied my background is. First, my name is Petronius Frisk, not Jacob Larson. That's one thing." He had decided to tell Miss Driscoll almost the whole story.

"You said you spent a year in the seminary?" she prompted.

They sat at a corner table in the tea room of the Occidental Hotel. She inclined her head to listen, cheek resting against the palm of her hand. Petronius had tucked his damaged arm below the marble top of the table.

"I didn't think I had the call to be a priest, but Father Brubacher, the head of the orphanage, wanted me to give it a try. He'd helped me a tremendous amount so I agreed as a favor to him. I did fair enough on the studies but got into trouble with my wrestling and brawling. All in fun it was, but didn't fit the rules. They asked me to leave after a year."

"They probably realized you didn't have the call."

"That became my occupation for a time after I left the seminary, brawling I mean. Prize fighting actually. I proved myself rather a good boxer. That's when I took the name Petronius, a Roman emperor I'd come across in my Latin reading. A name like Petronius gave the boxing fans the idea of a foreigner, a gladiator even. Added a little extra to the advertising card."

"What's your given name?"

"Peter, it was. Peter probably better suited me in the boxing ring. Even though I won most of my bouts I didn't satisfy my manager. He said I lacked the killer instinct. Couldn't finish off a hurt opponent."

"To me that's an admirable lack," she said.

"About then I noticed some men making a living playing professional baseball. That had been my favorite sport at St. Ignatius and the seminary, though neither school had an organized team. I could hit and throw but I needed a lot more experience. I played for a couple of small teams and then got a try-out with one of the better amateur teams in the police league, from the yards precinct."

"What do you mean by the yards?"

"That's an area in south Chicago, mostly stockyards and slaughter houses. After they saw me play, they wanted me on the team bad enough to give me a job as a patrolman. That way I wouldn't be a ringer, and against the regulations. Funny thing, the police took their baseball serious and played by all the rules. Now their regular police business, that was different. Well it wasn't long before I was the best player they had, both batting and pitching. And a couple of other teams began talking to me, trying to lure me over. My precinct gave me a promotion to detective to be sure I'd stay. A mistake that was, me taking the promotion."

"You didn't like being a detective?"

His voice rose a pitch in intensity. "I liked the thinking part of detective work well enough. But at the same time I got a closer look at the inner workings of the force and all its shady business. The health officer for the slaughter houses was a man from my own department. Of course he didn't do any inspecting. He just collected bribes from the worst offenders. The hardest part of his job was convincing the higher ups they were getting their proper share of the bribes."

"How terrible," she said.

"I got in the middle of investigating some poisoning

deaths. Turned out to be spoiled meat from one of our packing plants, and that plant owned by one of the richest men in the city. We were told to find another explanation for the poisonings. Money changed hands. I could have had my share but didn't go along. First thing I know I'm knocked back to patrolman. Well, I was bullheaded enough to go to the police commissioner with my story. That got me tossed off the force entirely. That's where I should have let it lie. I should have walked away and played baseball. A couple of the minor league teams were starting to show some interest in me by then."

He finished off his coffee before continuing. "But my blood was up and I went to one of the newspapers thinking what I had was front page news. The story never got printed, and two men came after me with clubs."

"Oh, my!"

"My boxing experience helped. In fact I had them both down on the ground. I should have finished them off right then and thrown 'em into the river."

"I'm so glad you didn't," she said with some spirit.

"But because I didn't finish them off I got thrown in the river myself. My arm caught a piling on the way down. I managed to pull myself out of the river and get to the hospital but the doctors couldn't save my arm."

They sat in silence for a time. "You did the right thing," she said quietly.

He replied with some heat, "If I'd known the cost I wouldn't have done it."

"It is a terrible cost," she agreed.

He pulled up his bad arm and banged it on the table. "I could be playing baseball for one of the professional teams if I had two good arms."

She nodded her head in sympathy. "What did you do after your injury?"

"Tried to find work. But I was blacklisted, sort of like

your father and his Muskegon Club friends. I did get one job with a detective agency but they gave into the blacklist pressure and let me go."

"Then how did you happen to be hired by the insurance companies?"

"My friend from the police force, Jacob Larson, left Chicago for the West. Said he wanted to live the cowboy life before it was all gone. I asked him if could I use his name and background to get work, and he said I could. He and I resembled each other well enough, though he was a better detective. I had to tell the insurance companies some stories about this bad arm. In fact I put it in a sling and made believe it was a slight fracture. I also padded my experience investigating fires."

"Why didn't you leave Chicago also and start fresh somewheres?"

"I like Chicago. Exciting place to live. Fastest growing city in the world did you know?"

She grinned. "Oh, we hear that all the time."

What he didn't tell her was his intent to return to Chicago and settle scores. His plans were still a little vague in that direction. He knew he needed to amass some capital to fight the big men.

"Is it possible that all the intrigue you see around you now is a result of your past adventures in Chicago? Could there be a connection?"

"Might be, but can't say I see it. Do you? Can you puzzle it out?"

"I can't," she admitted. "So what have you learned about the McClatchen fire?"

"The latest news is the night watchmen have left town. Probably McClatchen's doing. He doesn't want them in court being jabbed at by some crafty lawyer from the insurance company."

"Won't their leaving make McClatchen's case look even

worse?"

"Can't look much worse. Fire starting between 3AM and 4AM, just like the Michigan Shingle and Lumber fire. The watchmen claimed it was from a hot bearing on one of the saws, smoldering all that time until it finally flared up. Does that seem possible to you?"

"Embers can smolder in sawdust for a long time, but I wouldn't think for that many hours without some noticeable smoke or smell."

"A water hydrant was right there in the mill but the watchmen never got the hose hooked up. Said it tangled hopelessly. Claimed they threw a few buckets of water then turned in the alarm. Not much the fire company could do by the time they arrived."

"Yet McClatchen must feel he can still win if he's going to court."

"That's why the insurance companies wanted the hearing moved to Grand Rapids. McClatchen isn't such a big man there. But I expect he'll exert every pressure he can."

"Will you be testifying at the hearing?"

"The McClatchen fire was all over and cleaned up before I arrived, so I couldn't offer much. Also I don't want my lack of experience showing. I'd look pretty silly in front of those lawyers."

"So what are your immediate plans?"

"My plan is to protect the insurance companies against arson fires." He didn't tell about the large bonus awaiting him if he held things together over the next year. He meant to win that bonus at all costs. "My first step," he went on, "is to find out which saw mills are ripe for fires."

"How do you intend to do that?"

"Hoped you could tell me. If a lumberman runs out of logs to cut what's he likely to do with his sawmill?"

"He could contract with one of the others to saw their surplus logs. Of course that would only work temporarily."

"What other possibilities?"

"He could dismantle his mill and ship it by train to the forests west of here. A couple have already done that."

"But if the equipment were old wouldn't he be tempted to travel west with just the insurance money?"

"Most mills contain both old and new equipment. And it would depend on the final destination also. Wisconsin and Minnesota have white pine forests similar to Michigan's and the same mill equipment would work fine there. But the trees in Oregon and Washington, which are mostly fir and redwood I understand, grow to such huge diameters that larger saws and shuttling tables would be needed. So yes, if he was headed to the far western states his present equipment would be of little use."

"Then what would he do?"

"I suppose just sell his mill for whatever money he could get."

"Is there much of a market for used sawmill equipment?"

"Not around here, with the lumber business winding down. There are machinery brokers in Chicago, but unless the equipment was of the most modern design I expect it wouldn't bring much."

"I've another idea. It would be nice to have an informant at each mill. Any you could suggest?"

"The night watchmen obviously."

"Ha! The likely culprits of the fires so far. Who else?"

"I'll need some time to think about it," she said. "Oh, should I address you as Petronius Frisk now?"

"We'd best stick to Jacob Larson if I'm to keep my job with the insurance companies."

They each paid their own checks and departed the tea room. Petronius said he would keep her apprised of events.

THE RIGHT TRACK
Those citizens who are trying to develop and settle Muskegon County's available farming lands are on the right track. Such a growing city should not have rich lands unused at its very doors.

Muskegon Daily Chronicle

Ch 7

Petronius took the early train to Grand Rapids and was at the land office as the doors opened. Being the lone customer he was given the full attention of the chief registrar, in fact more attention than he preferred. The registrar brought over a plat book, took a seat and began talking.

"It's quieted way down," he offered. "Many a morning there'd be a half dozen, even a dozen men ready to run in as soon as we threw open the doors. And not just run in either, determined to be the first in. Grabbing each other's arms, kicking ankles, behaving no better than bar toughs. Important businessmen these were, some having traveled all night by wagon or horseback and looking wild and disheveled because of it. All with wads of cash in their pockets and all thinking the others might be after the same sections of timber."

At first Petronius tried to show interest but it quickly became apparent there would be no end to the stories. He found himself responding only with faint grunts and nods as he scanned the records.

"I can't say it didn't make me and my office feel important at times, even when my life was in danger. One gentlemen was so hurried and flustered he named the wrong township and only realized it when a pair of men right behind him bought the very land he thought he'd got for himself. He tried to fight them at first and then went for me, demanding I set right. On the floor over there, that's where we wrestled, me and him and two clerks, with him going for my throat and the clerks trying to pull him off. The sheriff didn't arrive any too soon."

Gradually Petronius grew accustomed to the distraction and was able to concentrate on section numbers, townships and range designations. Miss Driscoll had given him instructions on how to scan the land records and what information to record.

"Only once did we experience actual gunfire," the registrar went on. "And that was in the way of celebration. Fella gave a whoop and put three bullet holes in the ceiling where you see that patch. Couldn't even wait until he got outside. A lot of celebrating went on here. One time a man jumped over the counter and embraced me after he'd bought his land. Wanted me to leave all my work and join him in a fancy dinner at the Bancroft Hotel. When I couldn't do that he tossed me a $10 gold piece."

Throughout the rest of the morning Petronius caught snatches of stories as he went through page after page of records.

"Wished at times I could be the one all excited and celebrating my good fortune---Went land looking myself once in the north woods---Could have taken bribes---Had opportunities."

Petronius worked right through the lunch hour. Then with two plat books still to go he checked his watch and discovered the time was near for the McClatchen court hearing. He hurriedly asked directions to the court house and set off at a fast walk.

The court room was a large one, made somber by dark wood paneling and too few lamps. About 15 others occupied the visitor benches. Petronius entered the room quietly and planted himself in a back corner. He kept his hat on and also put a newspaper in front of him, as if he had come in mainly to read.

The proceedings had already begun as a man in a fire official's uniform answered questions from the witness stand. He was a thin fellow with a shaving brush of a mustache.

"The fire was ripping away by the time our company got there," he said. "We was reduced to what you might call spectators like everyone else. We did save the piles of lumber on the docks."

"What was the reason for your delay in reaching the fire," asked the questioner, evidently a lawyer for the insurance companies.

The man on the witness stand seemed genuinely offended by the question. "No delay at all on our part. The firehouse you know is only seven blocks away and mostly down hill to the lake. We didn't get the alarm until late."

"What reason was given for the late alarm, sir?"

"Night watchmen said they thought they could douse the fire with their own hose. Claimed they tried to work too fast and got it all tangled. Only when they saw the hose was hopeless did they call us."

"Does that explanation make sense to you?"

The fire official pursed his lips, hesitated and slowly shook his head. "Don't take but half a minute to turn in the alarm."

The lawyer nodded in agreement. "With your considerable experience with fires would you say this blaze was of an incendiary nature, that is deliberately set?"

Before he answer, another man, obviously the McClatchen lawyer, popped up to protest. Rapid words were exchanged and the judge banged his gavel. When quiet was restored the one who had lodged the protest addressed the fire official. "A single question to you, Fire Chief. Did you find any evidence the fire was deliberately set?"

Sawdust Fires 43

"Wouldn't be none would there, if a man just tosses a match to a pile of sawdust?"

"That isn't what I asked. Did you find any evidence of a deliberately set fire?"

"No, sir, I didn't but...."

"That's all."

While the witness returned to his seat the judge inquired as to the presence in the courtroom of the night watchmen. Though a slight man with thick spectacles, the judge cast a wonderfully clear voice throughout the room.

After a suitable pause the McClatchen lawyer stood, saying the men had apparently left the area and no one had knowledge of their whereabouts. He announced Mr. McClatchen would be disposed to testify in their stead.

The man who next took the witness stand came close to Petronius' picture of a lumberjack; tall, wide-shouldered and gaunt. The only thing which worked against that image was the man's age, which Petronius put at something over 60. He didn't wear the lumberjack's rough clothes but the suit he had on looked rumpled enough to have been slept in.

He gave his full name as Angus Ramsey McClatchen, swore his oath on a Bible which he said had belonged to his mother in Scotland, and then sprawled in the witness chair, one leg folded comfortably over the other. His clean shaven face was dominated by big tufts of eyebrows. It was a stern face but grandfatherly too. A strong head of hair, likely red once, but gone grey and frizzy, topped a tall forehead.

"Mr. McClatchen," began the insurance lawyer, "are you familiar with the details of the earlier fire at Michigan Shingle and Lumber Company?"

"I read of it, laddie, in the paper." He spoke his words with a strong slow voice and with some burring of his r's. At times he raised or lowered his voice as if for effect.

"What was your impression?" the lawyer asked.

"I thought about fires being a constant risk to all of us in the lumber business."

"Did you also consider the circumstances of that fire to be suspicious as mill fires go?"

McClatchen slapped his hand down on the railing and turned to the judge. "Aint I here to answer questions about my own fire?"

The judge agreed that was so and made the same suggestion to the lawyer.

"Well, fine," the man went on unperturbed. "How do you think the fire started in your own mill?"

"Most likely a hot bearing caused it, like the watchmen said. Or else one of 'em was smoking and dropped some hot ash. Maybe that's why they run off."

"Do you allow smoking in your mills?"

"It's agin my orders."

"Had these men any history of disobeying your orders?"

"Laddie, why don't you just ask whether I set the fire. That's what we're all here to settle, ain't it?"

"Very well. Did you order that fire set or have any knowledge of its being set?"

"No, I dinna. Nay to both of them questions."

The lawyer took a few paces away before turning again to McClatchen. "Is there anything you could add to truly convince us? You have a reputation, after all, of being uncommonly– what's the word-- unyielding in affairs of business."

"I would have done a smarter job of it."

"Ah." The questioner brightened. "How would a smart man have gone about it?"

"I'd have to think on it some."

"But at least you admit the fire could have happened in a less suspicious manner?"

McClatchen ignored the question and turned again to the

judge. "If I dinna set the fire, the insurance money is due me. Is that not the fact of it?"

"If the court can determine you had nothing to do with the fire then, of course, the insurance companies are held to the terms of their policy," the judge stated.

McClatchen took up his mother's Bible again. "I done things in business some men have called mean, but I dinna ever break a sworn oath." He placed his hand on the book and repeated his denials, then looked to the judge as if the matter were ended.

The lawyer, not entirely sure how to proceed, also looked to the judge.

"Mr. McClatchen, if you can't be bothered with any further inquiry here my decision rests with the insurance companies."

"What are ye saying, laddie? That I'm a liar?"

"I have known people to lie in court, sir, even after taking an oath."

"Are ye sayin' that I am?" McClatchen challenged with considerable heat.

The judge remained uncowed but seemed to strain to keep his voice calm. "I'm saying the fire could very well have been of an incendiary nature. Substantial questions remain here. It would be helpful to this court, for instance, to hear the accounts of the night watchmen. If you can produce them I'll gladly take up the matter again. Until then this court is adjourned." He struck his gavel on the bench with a little added wallop.

"If that's what most bothers ye, I'll announce right here the amount of $1000 to whoever brings in one of 'em and $3000 for the pair."

The spectators made little sounds of wonder at the size of the rewards but the judge took no notice as he moved quietly out of the courtroom. As McClatchen moved to confer with his lawyer, Petronius slipped out. In spite of the dramatics the proceedings had gone predictably enough, he thought.

He returned to the land office and finished the remaining plat books before the clerk shuttered the office for the day. There was just enough time to catch the evening train back to Muskegon.

The passenger car was only half full so Petronius had a whole seat to himself. He used the space to spread out his supper of a leg of chicken, rye bread and a bottle of milk purchased at the station. His appetite made the plain fare taste unusually good.

After he had eaten he set out the pile of notes he had taken at the land office and worked at sorting the tracts of land by owner. What he had in mind was to find how much timber each lumberman had left. Miss Driscoll had cautioned him as to the difficulties. For instance a lumberman might hold options for future purchase of timber rights. Generally those wouldn't be of public record. Then there was the problem of determining how much of the land had been already cut over. If the taxes weren't paid you could be sure the land was logged and would be allowed to go back to the State. But some lumbermen continued to pay taxes on cutover land they thought might be valuable for farming or mineral rights.

After a half hour of effort Petronius settled back in his seat and pulled out a pamphlet on Muskegon furnished by the town's businessmen's club. He had only glanced at it before.

The name Muskegon came from a Chippewa word meaning "river with marshes." A trading post had been established some time early in the 1800s. The first sawmill had been built in 1837, the same year Michigan was admitted to the Union. The Great Chicago Fire of 1871 had given impetus to the lumber business, and now more than 40 sawmills ringed the lake, turning out 600 million board feet of lumber and 400 million shingles each year, "fully enough to build a wide road all the way to San Francisco."

The original great stands of white pine had stretched north from a line roughly between Grand Haven and Saginaw Bay. The Muskegon River ran nearly 200 miles through those stands, draining a basin of 2800 square miles and emptying into Muskegon Lake. Said lake was seven miles long and three miles wide, "forming the finest natural harbor on Lake Michigan, not excepting Chicago."

The city population had swelled to 28,000 with over 4,000 being employed by the lumber mills and another 300 at work for the booming company.

Counted among the city's most prominent citizens were Angus McClatchen, Martin Crisp, J. J. Talman and Morgan Detwiler. Those named gentlemen were not only wealthy lumbermen but "public spirited lights to their community" as well.

The booklet contained a good deal more praise, including the claim Michigan's lumber industry produced more wealth in a year than had all of the California gold rush.

After reading the pamphlet it was hard to find a reason not to live in Muskegon -- "no labor troubles -- two steamboats a day to and from Chicago -- connections with three railroads -- a climate both delightful and healthy!"

With those comforting words Petronius drifted off to sleep.

SHORTCOMINGS
For his shortcomings, the Indian has barbarism and a lack of opportunity to plead, but the vultures who feast upon him can fall back on none of those.

Muskegon Daily Chronicle

Ch 8

Petronius and Miss Driscoll were sitting in the sun room of her father's house as he reported the happenings from the Grand Rapids courthouse. The morning light streamed through the windows and spotlighted one side of the young woman's face, making it seem radiant and less scarred.

Petronius pointed out the large ad in the local paper. "McClatchen's offer of a big reward for the night watchmen is just for show I'd say. A bluff, nothing else."

"What does he hope to accomplish?"

"Influence the judge. But that man is as stubborn as McClatchen I'd guess, so things will stay as they are and no insurance monies will be paid out."

"You're pleased with how it went?"

"I am. Now, on to our next item of business. When are we heading up north?"

"Some time after Easter."

"I'd like to use the trip to see what timber is left and who owns it. That way I'll be able to keep the closest eye on mills about to run out of logs. I've got my notes from the land office organized."

"Your land office information will help but that's still a large order. We'll do what we can but---"

Petronius noticed a shadow. He looked towards the window and observed a brown face looking in impassively. He jumped to his feet.

Addy laughed. "You may résumé your seat. That's Sam Washoo who's a Chippewa Indian and does handy work for my father."

"What's he want?"

"His habit is to look in the windows of a house, see if anybody is home and then walk right in."

Soon a short, burly man in farmer's overalls and white shirt entered the room.

"Truly a good morning Miss Addy," he said. The voice was deep and he spoke his words slowly. The man had reached perhaps 60 years, though his ebony hair, parted mostly to one side, showed no grey. His face however contained deep creases and had a flat appearance, as if pressed against glass.

"Good morning, Mr. Sam," Addy replied. "I'd like you to meet Jacob Larson who has business in our town."

After the two men shook hands, Addy asked, "Has Joshua come with you?"

"Yes. But he waits outside. He has vowed to no longer enter the houses of white men for fear it will be taken as a sign of his servitude." The man's face gave no indication whether he viewed the situation with humor or seriousness.

Addy shook her head and gave a wry laugh. "Joshua is Mr. Sam's grandson. He's 13 now and in one of his moods. Most often we're friends, Joshua and I, but at times he counts me among the enemy."

The three of them went outside. A smallish Indian boy leaned against the wall of the house, his face made sullen by a scowling lower lip.

"Joshua," scolded Addy. "I'm disappointed in your logic. It would be more a mark of servitude if you weren't allowed in my house. And I've always made you welcome haven't I?"

"Don't always try to teach me lessons," he said in a pouty voice.

She laughed, not at all hurt by the remark. "Oh, I do, don't I." She pulled his head to her in a hug but he twisted away. He remained indifferent as Petronius was introduced.

They walked to the coach house, which had gables and towers similar to the main house, though on a smaller scale. Miss Driscoll pointed out some harness Sam was to repair. She also asked him to examine the horseshoes on a black mare.

"Now I have something for you Joshua," she called to the boy who had followed at a distance. "And I'll pay you good wages."

Joshua perked up noticeably. He asked questions as to the exact money involved and the nature of the work. When told it would be scraping paint on the house, he looked less pleased but still agreed to the job. She found tools for him and showed him a place to start.

Back in the sitting room Addy told Petronius that Sam would be accompanying them north as a chaperone. "I'd also like to bring Joshua along if you have no objections."

Petronius agreed. "Can't say I've ever met any Indians. Do many live in Muskegon?"

"Not anymore. I understand when the pensions from the treaty of 1836 were still being paid, over a thousand Indians lived in town or nearby. We did have an encampment along the Muskegon River a couple years ago. They hunted and fished for a month and then moved further north."

"Does Washoo do anything other than work for your father?"

"He and Joshua's mother have a little farm to the east, but it's not good land. The newspaper keeps saying the county has such rich soil, but from what I've seen it's all sand."

"Does the boy help on the farm?"

"Some. But he'd much rather hunt and fish. In fact he sometimes skips school to go off in the woods. I worry about Joshua. He used to be in my catechism classes but now he's stopped coming."

"You teach catechism at your church?"

"Yes, at St. Mary's, to a group of Indian children. I teach

them about Jesus of course, but also reading and writing and a few social skills. I want them to be able to adopt to our way of life as much as they can, as least the better aspects of it. Many resist that, more so than the teachings of Jesus and the gospels."

"They want to hold onto their old ways?"

"Yes. I'm sad their way of life is slipping away but I see no avoiding it. Especially when so many white people view the demise of the Indian cultures and even the demise of the Indian races as beneficial, in fact totally in line with Social Darwinism. Some of the Indian children can sense that attitude in white people. Joshua can, I know. He's told me about a dream of his, where a great flood wipes out all the white population and the country returns to the Indians and the Indian ways of 200 years ago. He says he welcomes the flood and prays for it."

"Such a flood would wipe out the Indians too wouldn't it?"

She gave a wry laugh. "I hadn't thought of it but I suppose that's true. Anyway I told Joshua it was an evil thing to pray for, as evil as the attitudes of the white men."

"To my way of thinking you might better be teaching the Indians to resist, to fight back in some way."

"But they can't win. The tribes in the Dakota territories who fought only brought more suffering on themselves."

"What's the best course then?"

"For my part I teach the children to read and write so they can prove they're as fit and as bright as the any of the white children. And I'm sure they are. And yet I see so many adult Indians choosing the worst of our ways, coveting the gaudiest trinkets and thirsting after liquor which can make them as crazy as the wildest lumberjacks. Such behavior plays right to the arguments of those who claim Indians are an inferior race."

"Sounds like you've got yourself an impossible job."

"Perhaps. I think the churches could help by reminding

their parishioners of what Jesus said about the least of his brethren. If we see the Indians as the least of Jesus' brethren then we owe them love. That's a message many of our prominent citizens don't want to hear. They're too busy acquiring wealth."

"The reason's simple enough," said Petronius with considerable conviction. "Wealth gives you the power to make and hold onto your way of life. You don't end up being the least of the brethren."

"That's true only if we assume this world is our final end. Do you believe in life after death?"

"Don't know." Petronius felt uncomfortable with the question and changed the subject. "So you'll make all the arrangements for our trip up north?"

"Yes. I think we'll be going the Friday after Easter, early. And speaking of Easter, would you care to accompany Mrs. Fogarty and I to Mass on Easter morning?"

"Thank you, but no, wouldn't care to. Your father won't be going with you?"

"He doesn't attend Mass anymore except for St. Patrick's day. It has to do with my mother's passing. When she fell sick my father apparently made a bargain with God, which of course didn't work out because she died."

"What was the bargain?"

"I don't know. All he said at the time was he wouldn't be reneged on, not by God or anybody."

"We'll, my own reasons are somewhat different and I won't trouble you with them."

"It would be no trouble if you cared to tell me."

He shook his head. "One last piece of business. I want to move from the hotel into a boarding house to hold down expenses. Know of any good ones?"

"You'll want a fairly plush one I assume to maintain your image as a wealthy land buyer."

"Quite frankly my budget points me to a cheaper place."

His recent losses at card games furnished another reason, but he wouldn't trouble her with that either.

She considered for a few moments. "Mrs. Charlton's house on Morris Avenue is cheap and clean I understand. Lots of mill hands stay there."

"That would be fine. I might hear news too about what's going on at the mills." He got up to leave.

"Wait," she said. " I have one last piece of business also. Would you be willing to come to the house on Easter afternoon for my annual Easter egg hunt? It would be a great favor to me. My father has helped in the past but now he chooses not to. I've also asked Joshua but I can't be sure he'll be there. He says such affairs are too childish for him now. I have the Indian children over and some of the neighborhood children and it would be such a help to have another adult."

The idea didn't appeal to him greatly but he agreed to help. She told him the time and he took his leave.

MANGLED

John DeWitt, a young man 22 years old, whose home is in Ferrysburg, while working in the night run, fell on the table of the slab slasher and into the saws. His right arm was cut, severing the bone. In his struggles to roll off the table, his left leg just below the knee was terribly cut.

Muskegon Daily Chronicle

Ch 9

Mrs. Charlton, the operator of the boarding house, exuded friendliness and joviality. She interspersed jokes and laughs with the rules and features of the establishment. Her boiler-like body also exuded heat apparently, making her face red and sweaty in spite of the relative cool of the day. The stair treads squeaked and sagged as she clomped upwards, leading Petronius to a room with three bunk beds.

"You won't mind sleeping with our best snorers will you? 'Course not. Snore right back at 'em I say." She again laughed.

The atmosphere of a boarding house was nothing new to Petronius. He had lived in boarding houses in Chicago. A good many single men did the same, unless they had wealth or close family.

Supper time found 19 other men, mostly in their 20s and 30s, gathered at a long table. Newspapers served as tablecloths. Although the mill workers had washed at the water basins in the basement the smell of the day's sweat almost overpowered the aroma of mashed potatoes and pork.

Before Mrs. Charlton and her daughters brought out the main food platters, Mr. Charlton, seated at the head of the table, started the meal with a silent bowing of the head for ten seconds. The tall, skinny man had the use of only one arm, the other gone due to a mill accident. He let the empty sleeve dangle loose at his side and seemed not embarrassed by his handicap. Nor did he ask for any deference from his wife or the others at the table.

Though silence was not ordered at Charlton mealtimes, the race to consume food served as a damper on talk. Mrs. Charlton had promised good food but not an endless supply. Now that her husband could no longer work, this establishment was the sole support of the family, and so the food budget would be held in tight rein.

Petronius was not a voracious eater but he rather enjoyed the fast pace and competition at the table. When extra portions remained on a platter the men raced to consume what was in front of them for a chance at another helping, all the while trying to maintain some appearance of table manners. That was a strict rule at Mrs. Charlton's table. All boarders would conduct themselves as gentlemen.

After the men had eaten Mrs. Charlton and her two daughters, already of considerable heft, ate their own meal at the table. A few card games also started up. Petronius remained on as an observer, thinking he might hear some inside news from some of the sawmills but the talk was only of bad luck with cards and sore backs from pushing lumber. Petronius did ask Mr. Charlton about his injury. The man told how his sleeve had been caught up by the machinery and his arm pulled into the consuming saws, giving a few more physical details than Petronius thought necessary. He told the tale without rancor or despair at his reduction in status. Mr. Charlton helped however he could around the rooming house, cleaning, filling water basins, stoking the furnace and running general errands.

The first night sleeping at Charlton's convinced Petronius he should put his name in for one of the smaller more private rooms. Though he had tried snoring right back, as Mrs. Charlton suggested, he couldn't hear himself in the general din. The total effect was not unlike the sound of a sawmill he imagined.

Petronius spent Easter morning walking. He started at the lake below the downtown and continued westward along the shore, looking at sawmills as he went. The day was cloudy but showed occasional breaks of blue sky.

The morning Easter services would be in full chorus by now, he thought. He could remember serving Easter mornings as an altar boy for Father Brubacher. The church would be lush with the smell and brightness of flowers and the priest would begin the Latin prayers with a loud and buoyant, "Introibo ad altare Dei, I will go to the altar of God." Petronius and the other altar servers would respond, "Ad Deum qui laetificat juventutem meam, To God, the joy of my youth." And later would come the special Easter prayers with all their alleluias.

All that was long past for Petronius now, a thing of his youth. In truth he felt a certain resentment towards Fr. Brubacher for not preparing him better for the hard realties of life, for painting the world a better place than it was. He felt lied to. Perhaps the feeling was unjustified. There had been no intention to deceive, certainly. Fr. Will, as he was called, was an unguarded optimist and believed the cheery stories and hopeful poems he spouted. And those were appealing to children. But looking back, Petronius thought he and the other boys would have been better served with cautionary tales of what lie ahead, a world of deceit and avarice.

Petronius reached the huge sand dune which separated Muskegon Lake from Lake Michigan. He began the slow climb, slipping back half a step in the soft sand for every one upwards. When he reached the summit the sharp wind coming off the water almost took his breath away. He paused at the top long enough to gaze towards Chicago, some 100 miles south and west across the lake, thinking he might spot its tallest buildings. But he could see only water. He sat down out of the wind on the Muskegon lake side. He could see the whole expanse of the town's lumber empire, the four dozen sawmills all quiet on this Easter day, the boat docks and anchored ships and lumber piles. So much of the water along the shore was rippled with floating logs, fenced into orderly squares and rectangles, that its surface looked somewhat like plowed fields.

The Easter dinner put out by Mrs. Charlton exceeded Petronius' expectations; juicy ham, baked potatoes, a tasty vegetable salad and hot cross buns for dessert. After taking a rest on his bunk he headed over to the Driscoll house and the scheduled Easter egg hunt.

The wind had diminished to a slight breeze and the sun had overcome the clouds enough to boost the temperature into the low 60s. Addy was entirely pleased by the turn in the weather as she had made lots of hard boiled eggs. Petronius saw a mixture of white and brown shells with a few already decorated.

"I leave most of the eggs uncolored," she said. "The children like the fun of dyeing them themselves."

Petronius was asked to hide two baskets of eggs, making them somewhat difficult to find but not impossible. He had no trouble locating hiding places in the park like grounds. Besides the gazebo there were a trio of ornate bird houses, numerous small fir trees and a rock garden complete with miniature castle made from small stones. He rather enjoyed the effort.

Addy next asked him to assist in wrapping little packets of candy in tissue paper. Those would be passed out after all the eggs were colored.

Many of the children arrived early and some had to be held back from beginning their search at once. By three o'clock, the official starting time, about 18 had gathered, mostly Indian children, though a few from the neighborhood also. Addy expressed disappointment more had not come from the surrounding houses. The two Stimson girls from the house across the oval were there at least.

The hunt was well underway before Joshua arrived. He made it clear he was too old to participate with the young children and yet he didn't seem anxious to help in any other way either. He just watched.

The older Stimson girl plunged right into the fray but the younger, a slight child of about five, stood off to the side, apparently frightened by the shouts and cheers of the older kids. A couple of times her sister yelled over, "C'mon Melissa!" and Melissa's legs would push her forward an inch or two but invisible cords held her from going further. Addy went to the child and whispered in her ear but that had little effect. The girl squinted her eyes, as if trying even harder, but still could not break away.

Addy came back to stand next to Petronius. "Melissa is so painfully shy," she said. "I hope she can overcome it or she'll miss so much that's wonderful in childhood."

"I began as such a child myself," said Petronius. "But I did force myself to get into things, like boxing and baseball. Those built my confidence."

"I'm happy it can be done," she replied. "I don't remember ever being shy myself as a child."

Just then Joshua held his arms straight out, as if imitating a great bird in flight. He swooped out, made a couple of soaring loops, then slowly dove, before pouncing on an egg he had spotted on the far side of the yard. He made one large ascending spiral to gain altitude, then coasted, swerving from side to side and wobbling his arms gently until he dropped down in front of Melissa. He formally presented her with the egg. She accepted it and said nothing, either from shyness or just fascination at his performance.

"Oh, that boy," said Addy. "Sometimes I could just hug him. As stubborn as he can be, there are things he understands I'll never understand."

Melissa still couldn't bring herself to join the other children in the search, but she held her egg and looked content, as if she had accomplished something. And later she took part in the egg decorating at the tables.

After the candy and punch had been distributed to the children, Addy pronounced the day rather a success. She thanked Petronius and invited him to stay for supper. He thanked her but declined the invitation. He asked her the time set for their departure for the north woods and then went on his way.

TREND

The quantity of logs transported to Muskegon mills over the last three years shows a clear and unmistakable trend downwards.

year	logs
1888	5,598,000
1889	4,708,000
1890	3,266,000

Muskegon Daily Chronicle

Ch 10

Petronius, Miss Driscoll, Sam and Joshua assembled early the next Friday at the Giddings Street depot. The train which was to take them north consisted of a three block long string of empty log cars and one special car at the very end. The locomotive, set to haul this arrangement, was of the Shay type, built for power rather than speed. Upright steam cylinders on one side of the boiler turned a long shaft which was geared to each of the dozen driving wheels. Joshua was allowed to climb into the engine cab and inspect the fire box as well as pull the throttle and a few other handles. The boy had a few days left in his Easter vacation and so would miss no school, although he had no objection to missing school.

The special car was a general purpose affair, with most of the floor space set aside for carrying freight. Passengers had six wooden benches towards the rear with some small windows to look out. A short platform extended from the back of the car.

Petronius stacked his and Addy's suitcases atop some large barrels in the freight area of the car. Sam and Joshua had each brought their changes of clothes in feed sacks which they placed under their seats. Joshua also carried a box of fishing equipment which he kept on his lap.

They saw another passenger, a fellow with a scruffy beard, already seated. The man appeared to be in his mid 50's and had an angular frame which made him look all elbows and knees. His trousers stopped well short of his ankle high boots, exposing shins covered with bumps and scars, more bark than skin.

"Hello, Mr. Wanagan," called out Addy. She said it loud enough but the man didn't respond. What occupied his attention was a stick he was whittling with short quick strokes, building a pile of shavings between his feet. But as the man whittled the stick took on no particular shape.

"Mr. Wanagan is a timber looker," announced Addy as she took her seat. "One who scouts out the best tracts of pine and reports back to a lumberman." She wore tan corduroy trousers and a heavy striped blouse. A small brimmed hat with artificial flowers made her look womanly in her otherwise mannish attire.

"I've tried timber looking myself," she said to Petronius. "You can't imagine a harder job. Besides having to tramp over great areas and sleep in the woods, you have to know surveying and be able to locate section markers. Just finding a good stand of pine is hard enough, especially when the forest has a mix of oaks and maples and hemlocks. I've heard of old timers who claimed they were guided by the sound of the wind in the tree tops to some of the biggest stands of pine."

"Sound of the wind?" asked Petronius. "Why can't they just look? Use their eyes? Pines look different enough from oaks and maples."

"You'll learn when you get into the deep woods," she said. "Anyway, once a timber looker has located a good stand of pine he must place it precisely on a grid map so the lumberman can purchase the right acres. Next he needs to estimate the yield in board feet of lumber, and also gauge the difficulty of hauling the logs out of the woods. And all that has to be done accurately if the enterprise is to pay off." She looked over again at Wanagan. "I have a sympathy for that type of life. I wasn't able to put up with the mosquitos and deer flies and other hardships, but I liked the solitude and the feel of living in the woods."

"Speaking of timber looking, will we be able to get an accurate idea of what's left and who owns it?" asked Petronius. "I've brought the lists I compiled at the land office."

"We couldn't begin to, not even in a month. There are too just many square miles to cover."

Petronius could feel the anger rising in him. "Then what's the point of me going on this trip? I'm certainly not about to buy your father's cutover land."

"You'll get a good look at a lumber camp and a stand of pine. That's important in learning about the lumber business."

He shook his head. "What I want to learn is which mill owners have timber and which are about to run out."

"I'm sorry," she said. "Perhaps I misled you. My enthusiasm sometimes gets the best of me. I must admit I like this lumber business-- as rough and plunderous as it is. I can't help but feel there's something grand about it. There are times I'd like nothing better than to be its tour guide and show everyone the whole of it while it still exists in our State."

Petronius didn't answer and Addy returned to her sketch in some embarrassment. Just then, with a clumsy motion, Wanagan got to his feet and went out onto the car's platform. Joshua ran to watch as Wanagan began to pee off the back of the moving train.

When Addy saw the man was to be on the platform for a while she turned to Petronius. "Everyone calls him East-West Wanagan. His habit is to go east in the morning, jog north at mid-day, then follow the sun west until nightfall. East-West Wanagan." She couldn't repress a giggle. "He walks steady and covers an area thoroughly but apparently doesn't have the intuition or luck of the best land lookers. At least he hasn't

Sawdust Fires   63

gotten rich as many have."

Wanagan returned to his seat, showing a pronounced limp. Addy studied her sketch for a time and then excused herself. "I'm going to speak with him."

She sat down beside Wanagan and they talked earnestly for several minutes. Then she came back to Petronius. "Mr. Wanagan has fallen on very hard times. Do you have some money I could give him?"

Petronius reluctantly pulled out a bill.

"More. I promise you the money will be well spent." She took the cash, drew out a notebook from her bag along with some maps and returned to Wanagan's side. For over two hours they conversed, with Addy doing a lot of scribbling in her notebook and Wanagan pointing to spots on the maps. Petronius read from his copy of the Police Gazette, updating himself on the world of boxing and the upcoming season of professional baseball. He also watched the passing scene. He saw lots of fields where all the trees had been cut out to the horizon. Occasionally a narrow gauge spur railroad angled off into the hills towards some distant lumber camp.

The train stopped at a small town to drop off some freight and pick up a couple more passengers. Wanagan quickly got off and hobbled up the street, perhaps looking for an open saloon and a fast drink.

Addy put her notes and maps in some order and then began to answer the question that was on the others' minds.

"Timber lookers are usually as close-mouthed as spies. But Wanagan's had an accident. He fell on some rocks this past winter and injured his leg. Since he wasn't near any town he didn't have it looked to promptly and his leg stiffened to the point where he was crippled."

"I've got something in common with him there," said Petronius

"He's been in Muskegon spending all his savings on what he calls quack doctors," she continued. "None of them could repair his leg and now his timber looking days are over and he has no money."

"What's he been telling you about the maps?" Petronius asked.

"He's pointing out where the standing timber remains and his estimates of the quantities. We just finished going over Clare County. Of course he's been over almost every section in those northern counties and seems to have a marvelous memory for it all. That's the very information-- Wait, he's coming back. I'll tell you more later."

Wanagan, apparently frustrated in finding what he was after, slumped back into his seat. Addy rejoined him and they took up their discussions again. After another two hours of effort Addy folded all her maps and returned to her place beside Petronius. She looked very pleased with herself.

Obviously Wanagan had been more successful at the train stop than first appeared, as he pulled a bottle out his pocket and began taking healthy swigs. After a half hour he began to nod off and then snore through his nose.

When Addy was satisfied Wanagan slept soundly she took up the story again. "What has made him so bitter and so talkative is the treatment he's received from Mr. Talman. Wanagan worked for Mr. Talman for nearly 25 years and, according to Wanagan, was the most honest and loyal employee any lumberman ever had. Wanagan says he never set aside any plots of timber for his own purchase as most timber lookers have. In return for that loyalty Mr. Talman promised him he'd be well taken care of should his timber cruising days end prematurely. Now that the time has come to collect on that promise Talman has only offered him a laborer's job in one of his sawmills. Wanagan wanted at least a loan so he could start his own trading post up north, but no matter how he argued Talman wouldn't give in. They almost came to blows."

Sam asked, "What does he intend to do to live now?"

Sawdust Fires 65

"He could probably get a job as a log scaler or at least a cook's helper but he'd rather be his own boss. He thinks he'll become a shacker in the Upper Peninsula."

"Shacker, what's that?" asked Petronius.

"An individual who lives in a little house in the woods provided by one of the lumber companies. He cuts small timber and turns it into fence posts and railroad ties, getting paid by the piece. It's a lonely life but that should suit Wanagan. Very little money can be made doing it though. That's why he was so grateful for the cash of yours I gave him."

"Was it well spent as you said?"

"Yes indeed. If you'll give me those notes you took at the land office I believe we can come up with a fairly good picture of the remaining timber and who controls it."

"That would suit me just fine," said Petronius.

"Don't expect it to be perfect. I'm sure even Wanagan's memory isn't that good. And tracts of timber can change hands quickly in the lumber business."

Petronius accepted those qualifiers easily enough.

Towards evening they stopped at another small town. All the passengers got off the train to stretch their legs except Wanagan, who slept on. Addy had hoped they would have time to get something to eat but the train crew said they intended only to drop some freight, fill the locomotive with water and head on.

Back on the train Addy passed out four small sandwiches. Then she and Joshua worked on an illustrated reading book she had brought along.

It was well after dark when the train entered Missaukee County and reached the siding reserved for the Driscoll logging cars. The four visitors made the two mile hike to the camp in under a half hour but still too late to wake the cook for supper. They would have to wait until morning to assuage their hunger.

Sawdust Fires 66

Addy was lodged in the camp office with a hanging blanket separating her from the quarters of the foreman. Petronius, Sam and Joshua were given beds in the bunk shanty and a choice of mattresses-- those stuffed with straw or ones containing pine needles. Petronius chose the pine needles.

FAST
Cut as much as you can as fast as you can!

Motto ascribed to Michigan lumbermen

Ch 11

Saturday was a regular work day for the loggers. Visitors, if they wanted breakfast, had to get up at 5AM along with the rest of the camp. The newcomers were more than happy to rise early. They'd eaten nothing since the previous day's sandwiches on the train.

The cook house sprawled low to the ground, a building fashioned of logs with the bark still on. Rags had been stuffed in the gaps and corners. A dozen kerosene lamps hung from the ceiling and the air was thick with the steam of hot food and coffee. Petronius was surprised to see only a third of the tables occupied. He was about to question Miss Driscoll but she pressed a finger to her lips. Platters and pitchers were placed down for every six people. The choices offered were broad enough: coffee, tea, pancakes with gravy, salted pork, fresh bread, dried prunes and even baked beans. It was strange to see the men eating in complete silence, except for their occasional slobbering. Most finished quickly and went out.

Afterwards Addy said, "It's part of the lumberman's code. No talking at meals. As rowdy as the men can be they obey that rule like school children."

"Works to the camp's advantage does it?"

"Oh yes. It keeps meal times short and prevents arguments and fights."

When it grew light outside they could see the hills to the west reduced mostly to tree stumps. Sam shook his head in wonder, and said in his slow voice, "Where can all the animals of the forest go now?"

In answer Addy said, "It's called clear cutting. I don't agree with the practice but all of the lumbermen do it now. For years they didn't bother with the hardwoods or the smaller trees, but with the best of the pine stands gone they're taking everything."

"You must tell them to stop," challenged Sam.

"Oh Sam, what can I do? Who will listen to me?"

He was adamant. "Tell them. Stop them."

She shook her head and faced Sam with a look of embarrassment and helplessness.

"Is this camp cutting down trees now? asked Petronius.

She took up the new question as a welcome distraction. "No trees are being cut right now. That's why so few loggers are in camp. The ones here are doing cleanup, moving the last of the logs from the winter's cut to the river."

"We won't get to see trees cut down?" asked a disappointed Joshua.

"There will be other interesting things for you to do Joshua. Mr. Larson and I are going to ride horses to look at some timber. You and Sam can ride somewhere too if you like, perhaps to some fishing lake."

At Joshua's urging they went almost immediately to the stables. Some battered saddles were dug out of a stall full of harness, and the stable man selected four horses for them. Joshua informed the man he needed no saddle and would go bareback, even though he had ridden little, and that on a mule. When Joshua couldn't be argued out of his intent, the stable man chose a different horse, a grey which looked half asleep.

After studying maps, they divided up; Sam and Joshua heading towards a large lake while Addy and Petronius rode towards the northwest.

The day stayed cool and overcast. Petronius's horse trotted along steadily with a bouncing motion which made it hard to sit comfortably. On her horse, a dark brown draft mare, Addy seemed more at ease, her back held straight, her bottom sticking to the saddle.

Soon there was no trail to follow and Petronius had to concentrate on his horse's actions. If he didn't pull on the bridle the beast would head directly for a stump and then take quick side steps which almost tipped Petronius out of the saddle.

After nearly two hours of riding they reached a low area dense with woods. They spent another half hour looking for a range marker and then skirting the woods. Addy reined her horse and dismounted. "Time to count trees."

"All of them?"

"Of course not all of them. But enough to make an accurate timber measurement."

The forest she explained, was a mixture. Though about half pine, it contained lots of beech and hemlock, plus oak and maple. To estimate the value you first needed to know how many board feet of pine would result when the logs were at the sawmill.

She spread out a section map. "What I'd like you to do is walk a straight line north, counting the large red and white pines. When you reach the far side, jog to the west a quarter mile and come back through. I'll be doing the same thing, but on an east-west line."

She pointed out the different kinds of trees and gave a brief description of each. Then she headed towards the east.

Petronius began his march into the woods equipped with a compass, jotting pencil and Addy's small telescope. He had been further instructed to count just the best pines, the "fivers." A fiver was at least two feet in diameter and stretched up 80 feet or more before branching out with live limbs. Five perfect 16 foot logs could be cut from a fiver.

He was to walk as straight a line as possible and look 100 feet to either side of his path, thus surveying a swath about and acre in width.

The trees didn't go straight up like ship's masts as he imagined they would. Some bowed for no apparent reason. Others, though straight, went off at angles, perhaps shifted at their roots by strong winds.

The forest floor was a spongy brown mat of needles and leaves, fragrant with pine scent and moisture left from winter. Frequent hummocks bulged up as if bodies had been buried in shallow graves. Those, he had been told, were parts of trees or upturned roots, long decayed and covered over with forest droppings. Sometimes the hummocks ran into long ridges-- whole trees which had fallen years earlier and melted into the carpet floor.

It was a problem at times maintaining a straight line. A larger problem was picking out the white pines. In the dim light most of the tall trunks looked alike. The beeches, with their smooth hides were easy to spot. And the red pines had a flat loose bark, like flaps of leather. But the white pine with its strong gnarls didn't look all too different from the creviced surfaces of the oaks and maples. And then there were the hemlocks. Even when he got close he couldn't tell the hemlock from the white pine. He found himself craning his neck and peering 100 feet into the air with the telescope to check their needles. The hemlock needles were short, looking almost like fringes of green lace, while the pines had long wispy needles.

At one point he tried to look up with the telescope while still walking and tripped on a tangle of fallen branches. He broke his spill with his bad arm but still cut his chin on the end of a twig. He paused only briefly to wipe himself off and plunged on.

He could scarcely believe Addy's story about the timber looker who could tell by the sound of the wind in the treetops when he was near white pine. But if it were so, what a talent! To be able to stride along, keeping your eyes about you while listening for the certain hum the breeze made with

Sawdust Fires 71

the pine needles

When he reached the northern edge of the forest he threw himself down on one of the hummocks. It wasn't soft like a mattress, but comfortable enough for a short rest. He brought a handful of the dried pine needles close to his nose, crunching them between his fingers to inhale the still sharp pine fragrance. Being amidst trees centuries old gave him a sense of well being, and even permanence. That in spite of having ridden through miles of former forest now tree stumps.

He closed his eyes and listened for the sounds of the woods. He heard nothing, not the slightest breeze in the tree tops, no cries of animals, not even the sounds of birds except for a single woodpecker hammering far away to the west. It was as if the forest was keeping still against an intruder.

About a half hour into his return route Petronius came to a clearing caused by a small marsh. At the far side he saw a pine of remarkable size. It started with a slight bend at its root but then went up like a huge flagpole 170 feet or more. Only a few frothy green branches clustered about its top, all of them well placed and shaped like banners flying in the wind. This pine lacked the symmetry of a Christmas tree, yet, to his eye, showed wonderful balance. He wanted to put up a sign saying, "Don't cut her. Leave this one for the ages."

As Petronius expected, Addy had reached their starting point well before him. She had put down a canvas for their meal of sandwiches and water and now reclined alongside, looking reasonably rested.

Petronius threw himself down on the ground with a tired grunt and handed in his figures. He had counted 287 pine fivers, but felt no exactness in his number. He was no woodsmen after all. But apparently the figure came close to her own tally because she immediately began to calculate on her writing pad. After some arithmetic she announced, "I estimate 8800 board feet of pine per acre."

"That's good is it?"

"Somewhat better than average." She did some more calculating. "Since I've measured about 3000 acres this tract should produce 26 million feet of pine and a like amount of hardwoods."

Petronius recalled some of the production figures for the Muskegon sawmills. "So this whole forest is barely enough to keep one sawmill busy for a season?"

"Quite true."

"But at least your father has a supply of timber for another year."

"He doesn't own this land. "He holds an option on timber rights. And to purchase the timber he'll have to come up with a lot of money, which I don't believe he has."

"So what's he going to do?"

"He could borrow, or he may just sell the option to another lumber company." Her voice took on a peevish tone. "I don't know his exact plans. As I've said before he doesn't really confide in me."

Petronius changed the subject by asking about the special tree he had seen. "Do loggers ever leave any of the big ones?"

"They cut them all, even the biggest."

"Survival of the fittest doesn't apply to trees?"

She ignored his sarcasm. "Of course it's rare enough when they find a six or seven footer, so they'll make it an occasion for posing and photographs. But trees aren't spared. Every tree will come down anyway, by wind or lightning or fire or rot, so they argue." She said this with resignation, but then her tone brightened. "There's a stand of 40 acres in the far corner of Newago County which belongs entirely to me. It's not heavily wooded but has some large trees. One pine in particular is my treasure; almost six feet in diameter and beautifully proportioned. I intend to make those acres into a park. I'll show you sometime if you wish."

"Sometime, yes," he mumbled. Right then he had no wish

to see more trees.

After they had eaten, both took short naps: Miss Driscoll with her back against a hemlock, Petronius stretched flat on the ground.

He would have slept longer but she woke him and suggested they get on with their work.

"More work? I thought we had only to ride back to the camp?"

"I want to map a line of travel for a rail line from here to the river."

"You're planning railroad tracks even before your father owns the timber?"

She slipped into her lecturing teacher voice. "Figuring the cost of getting the logs to the mill is as important as estimating the timber."

She had already set up a surveying instrument. At her direction he rode his horse to a far ridge and drove a wooden stake into the ground. They continued in this fashion, paying particular attention to marshy spots which might need to be bypassed or bridged. Miss Driscoll worked with her usual efficiency, and seemed to even enjoy the effort. Instead of taking the most direct route to the river they angled south a bit to reach a high bank.

"This is one of the major storage areas, where they pile logs to wait for the spring drive. It's exciting when they tumble them all into the river at once. Like an avalanche really. The men who knock loose the props have to be quick, and of course some make a game of barely getting out of the way in time."

"Sounds like something worth seeing, or even trying myself."

"More than once I've wanted to be right in the middle of it."

He observed the rapt look on her face. "You like so much of this lumber business and you're good at it. Surely you see yourself as a lumber baron someday?"

"Others have said the same, but there are parts I truly have no heart for."

"Couldn't handle the scheming and shady deals?"

"It makes me sound sanctimonious but I know I couldn't, not and still teach catechism to children."

They arrived back at the lumber camp after dark. Supper had long since been served and cleared away, however the cook had saved some stew and apricot pie. Petronius wanted to put his head down on the table as he slowly chewed his food. But Addy opposite him, also tired, sat up straight and lady-like.

Petronius dragged himself to the bunk shanty. He couldn't remember ever feeling so worn out and sore. Of course he wasn't in the same physical shape of his ball playing days.

Inside the building the smell of sweaty bodies and wet wool offended his nose but didn't keep him from heading straight for his bunk. None of the other men appeared ready to settle down. Tomorrow was Sunday and they could "stay in the hay" if they wanted. Some rinsed socks and Mackinaws and hung them on overhead wires. A pair of musicians pumped away on accordions, supposedly accompanying each other, but possibly playing different tunes. A half dozen men in the middle of the room played a game. One man closed his eyes, bent over and was hit on the behind with a board. The man struck then examined the faces of the others. If he correctly picked the culprit that man took his place.

Sam seemed to enjoy all the activity and air of celebration and tried to get Joshua to join in but the boy stayed apart, an angry look on his face. In any case Petronius quickly fell asleep in the midst of it.

SO MANY

It is suggested that every lumber camp have a register in which each employee can place his name, and that of his friends or family and their residences. So many men are killed in the woods each winter and no one knows where to write to give information.

Muskegon Daily Chronicle

Ch 12

Petronius woke early the next morning feeling stiffness in his back and legs, yet surprisingly well rested. He wanted a bath badly but guests got no preference over loggers in the Sunday bathing schedule. It would be well into the afternoon before he got his turn. He decided not to wait and instead hunted up a towel and headed towards the river.

The day was dawning bright with a mist along the ground which softened the clutter of stumps and pine branches. Just as Petronius was about to move through a grove of scrub oaks along the river bank he sensed someone already there. He slowed and advanced quietly. It was Addy, apparently just finished with her own washing. She was clothed in a light shift though her loose hair still dripped. If he had been 15 minutes earlier he might have seen quite a show. As it was he thought of announcing himself and making believe he had been there all that time to watch her bathing. He had to admit he would enjoy her embarrassment. But he couldn't bring himself to such an ungentlemanly act. He moved silently away and walked well upstream for his own bath.

Petronius occupied himself until breakfast by poking about the barns and equipment sheds. The quantity and variety of tools impressed him. He examined short axes and double headed axes; saws with small even teeth and saws with rough gap-toothed edges; sledge hammers with large flat heads and some with heads embossed like cattle brands; poles with spear-like ends and those with curved hooks; and as for chains, there was every kind and size imaginable.

Gradually the loggers began drifting out of the bunk shanty and busied themselves washing underwear and sharpening tools. Petronius overheard some of their talk and gathered that Joshua and his riding skills had become a great joke among the men. Apparently the horse he had been given was nearly unridable and bucked Joshua off at every opportunity. The boy had spent a miserable day picking himself off the ground and running after his horse.

Petronius told Addy what he had heard and after breakfast she tried to console the bruised but still game Joshua. He announced he wanted to ride again but this time with a saddle and a far better horse. But the stable man said the horses deserved a day of rest along with the men. Addy and Joshua argued with him but the man wouldn't yield. A few loggers heard the exchange and snorted in amusement. That sent Joshua into a deep pout and he went stomping off into the mist with Sam following and trying to calm the boy.

Addy grimaced and went to talk to the camp foreman. She also had conversations with several loggers.

"Some of the men have agreed to fall a tree for Joshua's benefit," she said at her return. "I suspect it's as much to show off as make amends for the prank. Either way Joshua should enjoy their little show."

After Sam came back with the boy in tow, four loggers gathered some equipment and led them towards the tree line over a mile distant. Addy brought along her sketch pad.

The tree which the men had selected measured a little less than two feet in diameter but stretched almost 120 feet high. One of the loggers stepped off a dozen paces and drove a stake into the ground.

"That's to give them something to aim at," said Addy. In thick woods they would have to drop the tree accurately to

Sawdust Fires 77

avoid smashing into standing timber."

A right-handed man and a left hander alternated quick but hard strokes at one side of the tree with their double headed axes. Big white chips began jumping out like popcorn. After what seemed like only two minutes the pair drew back and tossed their axes to the ground, leaving a 10 inch deep notch in the pine. The saw men then got into position on the opposite side of the tree. They set the edge of the saw blade at a spot on the bark higher than the notch and began whipping the saw back and forth in a frenzied motion which seemed certain to bind the teeth. But their action was so rhythmic the blade slipped into the wood with only the mildest ripping sound. After the saw buried itself in the tree the men paused and drove steel wedges into the slot behind the blade. Two more minutes of sawing produced a sharp pop. Petronius instinctively moved a bit more behind the sawyers.

"Timberrrr," yelled Joshua.

The saw men made four more fast strokes and stepped quickly back, to the sound of a continuous cracking. The top of the tree shuddered for a second and then gathered momentum. The upper branches proved little cushion as the tree slammed down hard. Petronius felt himself bounced off the ground a bit with the impact.

The tree had missed the stake by a good four feet and the axe men argued with the saw men, at first good naturedly and then heatedly about who was to blame.

"They compete ferociously," explained Addy. "It seems to be in their nature. Who can saw the fastest? Which man can chop down the most trees in a day? What crew can pile the log sled the highest? I'm sure it does make the work less tedious, but to me it's rivalry carried to an extreme and often dangerous. Of course the foremen and owners do everything they can to encourage competition because it increases production."

"Have to say I agree with the men," said Petronius. "I like

a contest myself, and to win at it is the most fun."

The ax men began lopping off branches on the downed tree and the sawyers starting cutting the trunk into 16 foot lengths. Joshua picked up an untended axe and whacked away at a large stump, pretending he was about to fell a tree.

Addy looked for another scene to sketch. She pointed to a hill on which grew a half dozen pines, widely spaced. A pocket of mist behind the hill reflected a ray of sun and set off the rich green of the trees. The pines they had looked at yesterday went up like huge broomsticks, bushy only at their tops. But these were shorter and spread widely, with branches starting almost at ground level.

"What are those, a different variety of pine?" Petronius asked as Addy seated herself on a stump.

"No. They're also white pine, but the shape they take depends on their surroundings. On that hill, with air and sunlight on all sides they can push outwards instead of just up."

Petronius studied the trees, and then Addy's rendering. The green splashes of the branches had been sculpted by the wind into airy brush strokes which her colored pencils and talent couldn't quite duplicate.

Soon a breeze sprang up, blowing away the remaining mist and fog, leaving the landscape clear but drab. Addy set down her sketch pad and put away her pencils. "I'll show you something I like to do," she said. She led Sam and Petronius to the top of the hill. "Do either of you like to climb trees?"

Sam grunted and shook his head.

Petronius hesitated at because of his bad arm but said, "I'm willing to climb if you are."

She pointed. "You take that tree and I'll climb here."

Petronius watched as Addy pulled herself onto the first branch and began picking her way upward. He tried to imitate her speed initially but quickly slowed, testing each hand position and foothold before making the next move up. His feet and hands became sticky with pine sap.

Joshua down below saw what they were about and came running up the hill. He picked his own tree and began scaling it. Sam remained on the ground, looking up at the three climbers with a face which for once gave away his amusement.

Addy reached the halfway point on her tree and kept going until she was in the high branches, a good 60 feet above the ground. She wrapped an arm about the tree, her face close to the bark, and gazed out at some far horizon as the tree rocked with the wind.

Petronius tried to climb just as high but his knees wouldn't let him. He wasn't good at heights. The swaying of the tree made him feel he was atop the mast of a sailing ship in rough seas. But after a time he found himself relaxing. The swishing of the wind did have a soothing effect and for a bit he closed his eyes and let himself be rocked back and forth. He could feel the fibers of the tree stretch and contract. At one point he even loosened his tight grip on the nearest branch but then almost lost his balance. Though quickly recovering he decided to climb down from the perch.

Addy stayed up another 10 minutes and Joshua was the last to descend.

On the walk back to camp Addy declared she was going to spend the rest of the daylight sketching the buildings and layout of the camp, although there was nothing very picturesque to any of it. "I have a real affection for lumber camps," she said. "One of the memorable times of my childhood occurred in a lumber camp. Not this camp but an earlier one in Oceola County. I was 10 years old and spent my Christmas vacation with my father that winter. A huge blizzard overtook us, starting in the late afternoon. I can still remember the wind and blinding snow such that ropes had to be strung between buildings to keep men from losing their way, although the distances were short. But I wasn't afraid.

Despite my father's warnings I made several trips to the barn and other buildings, holding onto the ropes and imagining I was exploring the north pole."

Petronius had no trouble believing she wasn't frightened by such things as snowstorms.

"By next morning," she went on, "almost three feet of snow had fallen and my father declared a holiday for the entire camp even though it was a weekday. I'm sure the other camps put their men to work digging out roads and trails. My father told the loggers they were free to do whatever they wished. Many became like children again. Several built a large snow fort for me with tunnels running dozens of feet. The blacksmith and his helper made four or five sleds which were crude and slow but could run into trees without damage. I believe most everyone went sledding including my father. He said it reminded him of his own childhood. I don't recall ever seeing him so relaxed and full of fun as on that day."

She stopped and looked around at the others in some embarrassment at how she had gushed on. Petronius assured her the story was worth telling and worth hearing.

Joshua was now walking beside her. His spirits seemed restored and Addy raised them further by telling him she would talk to the stable man.

"I'll see if we can't find you a good horse to ride this afternoon," she said.

The two of them walked arm in arm the rest of the way back to camp with Joshua proclaiming Addy as his good friend.

Sunday dinner consisted of an excellent venison stew, hot rolls and several kinds of pie. Petronius and his companions ate more than enough and then spent much of the afternoon napping.

LIE TO CHILDREN

The poetry of life is mainly a lie; but it is the enjoyable element after all. Lie to children. Paint the world as bright and happy as you can. Give them all the pleasant pictures of it you can. They will find its hard and practical character quite soon enough.

Muskegon Daily Chronicle

Ch 13

The next morning the four visitors got up early and followed some of the loggers to their work area. The day was overcast with a slight drizzle falling. Some of the men had oilskins to stay dry while others just worked in their wool mackinaws, depending on exertion to keep warm. Addy had brought along her sketch book with a canvas cover for its protection.

Petronius found the movement of the logs rather fascinating. An overhead series of steel cables had been strung high between topped off trees, continuing as far as he could see. Hanging from rollers on each cable was a block and tackle arrangement which permitted one end of the log to be hoisted enough to clear all obstacles. The log was then dragged by the horse a distance of about 100 yards, the length of the cable. Horse and log were then connected to the next cable in line.

"Moving logs by sleigh in winter is the preferred and easier method," said Addy. "But now all the lumbermen are trying out schemes for skidding logs over bare ground."

"They plan to log year around then?" asked Petronius.

"Some already do, but mostly it's to prepare for the west coast where they don't expect a lot of snow. Another method of transport is to hook the end of a log under the axle of a pair of large wheels. The axle has a wagon tongue attached so horses can be harnessed to it and the wheels are big enough-- as much as 10 feet high-- to roll over almost any rough ground. In the mountain areas they expect to build water flumes to shoot the logs down the hill sides."

They watched a few more logs being relayed down the train of cables and then walked over to the loading area where logs where being winched up a ramp onto railroad cars. This proved of only mild interest and they soon headed back to camp to prepare for their departure.

By early afternoon the rain had stopped and they hiked with their luggage to the railroad tracks. They waited more than an hour for the tardy train to come puffing up to the siding. Its accommodations were much less than they had enjoyed on the trip north. Besides a string of flat bed cars filled with logs it offered only an open, box-like equipment car with no seats. An awning did offer some protection in case of rain. They rode seated on piles of chain and tools.

"What do you think of life in a logging camp?" Addy yelled to Petronius over the sounds of the jolting train.

"I like the idea of living in the woods and working outdoors. If I had two good arms I'd try logging for one winter just as a test of myself. I believe I'd do fine."

"No men work harder than loggers. And it's quite dangerous what they do. Still most of them want no other life."

"What wages do they make?" asked Petronius.

"About $20 per month is standard. They also receive bonuses for logs cut."

"So a man might end the winter with what, $90 or $100?"

"Around that. And it's quickly spent in the saloons and brothels. That gives the lumbermen another reason to hold wages low. They say the money flows straight to the Sawdust Flats anyway."

Sixty miles down the line the train stopped to hook on another dozen log cars. The travelers hopped off and hiked

Sawdust Fires   83

with their luggage to the nearby logging camp, expecting to spend the night. "It's the code of lumber camps to offer a night's hospitality to all visitors," explained Addy.

The camp foreman, a bearded brawny man looked at them suspiciously. "Those two with you?" He pointed to Sam and Joshua.

"Of course they're with us," snapped Petronius.

"I won't have Indians in my camp," the man growled.

"And why is that?" asked Addy in a mild voice.

"The same reason I don't allow thieves and murderers in this camp."

"How can you say such a thing?" she said. "Have you every known any Indians?"

"I seen a few, drunken savages they was."

"I give you my word as Terence Driscoll's daughter that Sam and Joshua are as respectable as anyone you have here in this camp."

"That'd be an insult to my men wouldn't it? Your word--"

"Listen my man," broke in Petronius. "We aren't here to debate whether these two are as dainty as your fool loggers. We need a meal and a place for the night and we mean to stay. All of us!"

The foreman's voice rose to a menacing pitch. "My word goes here and I say clear out!"

Petronius sprang for the man but Addy was just as quick to come in between the two.

"No, stop it," she commanded. "We'll leave."

Through it all Sam's face remained impassive but Petronius could see Joshua's eyes burn with resentment.

When they had gotten free of the camp Joshua yelled with his mad-at-everybody voice, "What will we do now?"

Addy shook her head repeatedly and appeared flustered. When she had pulled herself together she said, "Sam and Joshua, I must apologize for this." She took a map from her bag, pondered over it for a minute and then shook her head again. "We're at least 15 miles from Evart and we'd be walking half the night even if we could find our way in the dark. We'll have to make some kind of a camp right here."

Petronius suggested they look for a flat car on the railroad siding. In case it rained they could use the car for cover.

They gathered some pine cuttings and found two train cars. After they had built some nests with the branches Sam sat down with a big "Ah!" He looked at Joshua and waved him over, as if inviting him into a privileged place. "It's good for the blood and good for the soul to sleep in the open with the stars," he said.

Joshua looked up at the dark sky. "There aren't no stars tonight."

"They are there, past the clouds," Sam answered.

When the rain resumed they were fairly well protected at first, but a wind came up and the drops began angling in on them.

"I noticed a tarp in the camp, covering some firewood," said Petronius. "I'll get it."

"Be careful," advised Addy. "Most camps have a watchdog or two."

Full darkness enveloped Petronius by the time he reached the camp. A faint light coming through the single window of the camp office provided some illumination and allowed him to orient himself. He moved in extreme slow motion as he edged towards the wood pile. The noise of the wind covered any sounds he made as he untied the tarp and rolled it into a bundle. He had an urge to hurl a piece of firewood through the window of the camp office but restrained himself and slipped away as deliberately as he had come.

The next morning they awoke cold and damp although the tarp had kept out the worst of the wind and rain. They would get no breakfast nor have a place to wash themselves. Though rumpled of clothes and hair Addy tried to present a cheerful disposition. She again apologized to Joshua for what had happened at the camp and put his hand on his shoulder. "Try to forgive that man won't you? This is the very thing Jesus was referring to when he said to return good for evil and to love your enemies. Do you remember we talked about that in catechism?"

Joshua looked unconvinced.

"It wasn't you being called a savage," said Petronius.

"I know that hurts," she answered. "I've been called names myself."

"There's times when it better to lick your enemies," went on Petronius. "That's the only way they'll learn a lesson."

"And what if they return the lesson?" she asked.

"The harder man will win out then."

Addy gave a sigh and turned to Joshua. "You haven't had much chance to use your fishing equipment. Would you like to choose our next destination, some lake perhaps?" She spread out her map on the ground. They consulted Sam but he hadn't fished any the nearby lakes and could offer no opinion. Joshua looked over the map and picked a spot.

They returned to the main track of the railroad and followed it south for more than an hour, then headed west. When they got to the lake shown on the map Joshua expressed his disappointment. It's shores had been denuded of timber and presented a desolate look. They continued walking west until they came to a smaller lake, marshy at one end. Light woods ringed the shore, mostly birch and poplars, with only a few pines. They drank from the water and found it sweet. Sam and Joshua cut some pine limbs for fishing poles, took off their boots and waded 20 yards into the lake.

Petronius and Addy sat on shore. The day was lightly overcast with no wind, and they could hear tiny splashes and gurgles from far out on the water. Addy pointed across the lake as a family of deer emerged from the woods and stepped gingerly to the water's edge to drink. Petronius leaned back thinking he would just close his eyes and listen, but he quickly fell asleep.

Sam and Joshua had caught only six bluegills and small ones at that, but the four travelers looked forward eagerly to the meal. Sam split the fish and put them on roasting sticks along with wild onions he had pulled from the marsh. He started a fire with some dried grass and sparks from a small flintlock mechanism. It had been taken from a pistol more than 100 years old, Sam proudly declared.

The roasted fish tasted flat to Petronius, but he ate slowly and carefully, wasting none of it. He was offered some seeds Sam had taken from pine cones but after chewing on them for a while spit them out.

Petronius and Sam started to nap again but Addy roused them. She pointed to her map. "There's a camp near Big Rapids I'm sure will take us because I know the lumberman who runs it. The distance is almost a three hour walk but if we start now we'll arrive before dinner. What do you think?" Though she presented the idea as a question, her own wish was clear. They headed south at a brisk walk.

The camp proved as hospitable as claimed, though none of the four looked the least bit respectable by then. They wondered out loud which was the most welcome, the large dinner of chicken and corn bread, a clean place to wash and change clothes, or the prospect of a warm bed. They headed for their bunks even ahead of the hardworking loggers.

The next day's logging train proved even more poorly equipped than the one of the previous day, having only a dozen loaded log cars and a small flat car for equipment and passengers. The arrangement suited Joshua well enough as he rode on the top of a pyramid of logs cowboy style, at least for a time. The rest sprawled on the flat bed car and tried to keep themselves and their luggage from sliding off as the train jolted and bumped along.

They arrived in Muskegon after dark, feeling sore and

exhausted and looking a lot like hoboes. Their good-byes were brief as they headed to their respective lodgings. Addy did promise Petronius she would assemble Wanagan's timber data into a useable list.

In the following several weeks nothing of great import took place. Petronius and Addy met several times for business and also for a couple of social forays, including an outing on the 4th of July. On that occasion they watched a balloon ascension and then a very amateurish baseball game. Afterwards Petronius and Addy pitched and batted the ball around by themselves. She proved surprisingly adept at the sport.

HIGHER PLANE

The modest and attractive lady typewriter has thrown a grace and charm over the office in which she reigns that has banished the profane and suggestive word to the bar room. Offices are put on a higher plane.

Muskegon Daily Chronicle

Ch 14

Petronius didn't see Addy Driscoll for a few weeks, and then she sent a note asking for a meeting. They gathered at a tea shop on Western Avenue.

"I have an idea who can keep watch for you over the sawmills," she said with a touch of triumph in her voice.

"And who's that?" he replied a little tartly. He hadn't been able to come up with any plan himself.

"The lady typists in the offices of the lumber companies."

"How would that work? Seems like it would be hard for someone not actually at the mill to know what was going on."

"Lumbermen are planners and schemers, always looking for the most profit. I can't imagine they wouldn't take certain steps ahead of time if they were planning arson. The women in the offices would be in a position to observe those steps."

"And what steps would those be?"

"Perhaps the removal of a piece of newer machinery from the mill, or the placement of the highest grade lumber away from the fire, or just a difference in routine when something is about to happen."

"You don't think the lumbermen would try to keep it a secret from their typists?"

"I'm sure they would. But if the women were given instructions on what to watch for they might find out those secrets. I'll have to give this some thought and prepare a list."

"You may have a good plan but I wouldn't know how to

set it up. Wouldn't have the least idea what to say to your women typists."

"I can talk to them and do the recruiting. I see many of them at lunch times."

"You're sure they'd go for something like this?"

"I'd have to convince them they wouldn't be just spies, that they'd be extending their own jobs and those of the mill workers, and, probably as important, preventing something illegal. I'm sure not all would be convinced. Some would be too loyal to their bosses. But even those, if they just reported what was being asked of them, might serve as deterrents."

"How much would I have to pay these typists?"

"Perhaps a small initial fee of $5. After that you'd pay only for information when they had something suspicious to report."

Petronius took several slow sips from his coffee and considered. "I'm willing to try this. When can you start?"

"I'll begin tomorrow. It will take a fairly long time to contact all the typists, since the meetings would best seem to be casual rather than arranged."

At the end of six weeks they could count 28 of the 42 sawmills as under surveillance by one of their woman typewriters. A few of the lumber offices had no female secretaries and weren't approached. Some of the women had refused, of course, but Addy's methods had been circumspect enough so no one was outraged. When Petronius informed the insurance companies about the network he had put in place they wrote back an approving letter.

The next month went smoothly, despite a series of false and trivial reports from the excitable Miss Dellinger at Bigely and Hearst. A failure to order new saw blades exactly on time, a rumor of empty water barrels on the roof of the mill, any sort of meeting which ran longer than usual, these were enough to produce a note of alarm from Miss Dellinger. Nor did the typist get discouraged when her information was rejected. She just resolved to be ever more thorough and vigilant. And her vigilance, along with the vigilance of the other typists, appeared to work. None of the mills caught fire.

In the last week of October Petronius was viewing a boxing match in the crowded upper room of the Steindler house when he was interrupted by Addy Driscoll. "I've been searching for you," she said, rather embarrassed at appearing in such a rough establishment. When she had drawn him out of the building she went on. "Sara Jamison came to me with some information. She's typist at A. O. Ernst Lumber and told me the regular night watchmen have been replaced by two new men, young fellows she's never seen before. Mr. Ernst met with them in his office for close to two hours."

"That sounds strange enough. Ernst must intend something."

"I thought so too and paid Sara from the funds you gave me."

"What's our next step?"

"I can think of nothing better than you marching over to Ernst's house and talking straight and hard to him. But whatever you say try to keep Miss Jamison's name out of it. She was fearful about what might happen to her."

"I'll do that." As he walked towards Ernst's mansion overlooking the lake he tried to compose in his mind the little speech he would give to the man, not wanting to sound overly dramatic or even silly. "Sir, I have every reason to believe you intend arson at your mill. Don't think you can get away it. Not while I've got my eye on you. The insurance monies won't be paid, that's for certain." But he needn't have bothered rehearsing. The housekeeper informed him Mr. Ernst had caught the overnight steamship to Chicago.

Petronius next made his way to the Ernst saw mill, intending to talk with the night watchmen. It was then nearly 10PM and quite dark. He found all of the doors to the mill locked. He proceeded to pound on one until a face looked through a dusty pane of glass nearby. "G'wan home!" came an angry shout.

Petronius yelled for admittance but the man must have mistaken him for a vagrant. He did look a bit derelict, not having shaved since the day before. He resumed pounding on the door but got no further response. He tramped around outside the building for some time, uncertain of his next step. He heard someone approaching and to his relief saw it was Addy riding on her bicycle. She was wrapped in a shawl against the cool night air.

"When you didn't come back I assumed you might be here. What's happened?"

He told her of what had transpired and asked her assessment.

"I don't know what to think. This may be just a false alarm, or the fire could be set to go this very night. Yet I can't imagine they would use the same methods as before. Mr. Ernst is no fool. He must know the insurance payments for the McClatchen and the Michigan Lumber fires have been held up in court. Perhaps he has some way of making his fire look entirely accidental and beyond suspicion."

"Any ideas how that could be done?"

"I can't think of any."

"Has the mill got a telephone so I could call the night watchmen?"

"No. Too much noise in a sawmill."

"What do the watchmen do inside there, other than keep an eye on things? Just sit?"

"Mostly cleanup chores. Also some maintenance of the machines, oiling and such. In general they prepare the mill for the next day's work."

After a further silence she said, "Well, I'm sorry I can't provide more help but I'm going home and to bed. Do you intend to stay on here?"

He did intend, though he wasn't sure exactly what good

that would do.

"You know where the nearest alarm box is, of course."

He said he did.

She noted his rather light coat. "Please take my shawl. It'll keep you from catching cold."

He accepted the garment with mumbled thanks and watched her go off into the night.

The lake front held quiet and dark except for a few street lamps. Demand for lumber was down and none of the mills was running a night shift. The only sounds were the wind and the bumping of logs in the mill ponds. Petronius took a quick walk around the building to warm his blood and get himself thinking. He had made up his mind some time back that any further mill fires would be judged arsonous. If that meant planting a kerosene canister in the midst of the smoking ruins he would do that. His bonus money from the insurance companies had to be won. But he wasn't sure how to proceed now the details had to be worked out.

He could get a kerosene can, even at this late hour. He had noted where Mrs. Charlton kept her reserve stock. But how to place it in the mill and when? Once the fire got going the scene would be swarming with firemen and observers. He couldn't be caught doing something so suspicious. The results would be calamitous: embarrassing questions, an investigation, possible word of his bungling getting back to the insurance companies. But if he took the safer route and planted the kerosene in the mill ahead of time there was every chance it would be detected and disposed of, especially if the arsonists delayed a night or two. Another possibility was to hide the canister along the outside wall of the building. But that seemed unsatisfactory as well. It would be far better if he could prevent the fire entirely.

The other fires had started about three in the morning, still more than four hours away. He sat down in the shadow of a shed and caught some sleep, the shawl pulled around him.

Sawdust Fires 93

When he woke he checked his pocket watch. It was half past two. He got up and stomped some feeling back into his feet. The night had turned quite cold. He had just made up his mind to create some racket to get the watchmen outside when he saw someone coming on a bicycle. It was Addy again.

"I thought of how the fire might be done," she said as she rolled up, a bit out of breath.

What's that you've got there?" He pointed to a tool in the basket of the bicycle.

"A wood drill. I'll explain in a minute. Remember I told you the watchmen prepare the mill for the next day's work?"

He nodded.

"One of their duties is to fire the boilers and get up steam before work begins. Some years ago a boiler exploded when the watchmen were careless, and it occurred to me a boiler explosion could be used to burn down the mill."

"Sounds dangerous to the watchmen."

"They'd have move to a place of protection, of course. I brought the wood drill so we can watch what goes on in the boiler room."

"You're planning to make a hole in the wall?"

"Exactly."

A window existed on the end wall of the boiler house but high up, and looking at the back of the boiler. Addy picked a spot on a side wall. "Wait, no, here is better. If we drill through this knot the hole will look natural." She looked uncertainly at his bad arm. "Should I do it?"

"I'll give it a try." He took the drill brace and struggled with it for a time but couldn't crank it properly. He was about to throw the tool down with an oath but she signaled for quiet as a horse and wagon plodded past on the street.

Addy took up the drill and slowly bored the a one inch hole. Petronius put his eye to it. "All dark now."

"They'll light the room when they start the boilers. We have about an hour to wait."

Sawdust Fires 94

They rested against the walls of the building, planning to stay alert, however both soon drifted off to sleep. What woke them was activity inside the boiler room.

Addy looked through the peep hole for some time before motioning Petronius off a ways to talk.

"They've got something on the safety valve, a wrench I think," she said.

"To explode the boiler?"

"I'm fairly sure of it. Let's sound the alarm." They ran to the fire box and pulled the handle.

"How far is the fire station?" he asked.

"About a mile."

Five minutes went by and then ten.

"Something's wrong with the alarm box or they're not responding," she said.

"Could you ride your bicycle up there?"

"I don't know if there's time."

"If I could get into the building could I turn the boiler off?"

She explained about releasing the safety valve and banking the fire as they ran back to the mill. They dragged a long board from a pile of lumber, hoisted one end and crashed it through the window of the boiler room. As Petronius scrambled up the board he yelled to Addy. "Go around to the front and pound on the door. Might distract the watchmen."

He knocked out the rest of the glass and put his legs through the window and fell rather awkwardly but on his feet.

Inside the room the boiler strained like a living thing, fire box roaring and creaks emitting from the iron skin. With a trembling hand Petronius took the wrench off the safety valve releasing a gusher of steam. He didn't recall the rest of Addy's instructions but turned every wheel and yanked every handle he saw. Then he pulled the cord to the mill whistle.

In a few moments a man charged in, cursing and hefting a

Sawdust Fires 95

club. The watchman flew at Petronius, swinging as he came, but the club clipped an overhead pipe and missed. Petronius dodged around the man and out into the mill proper. The other watchman was coming, a hook of some kind in his hand. Petronius saw a stairway and recalled Addy leading him up to the roof of her father's mill. Stumbling, feeling his way in the semi-darkness, he climbed the stairs, then a ladder above that. He could hear one of the men following. He found the hatch, popped it open and got out onto the walkway at the peak of the roof. The man with the hook came out also. Petronius dodged around several of the water barrels and then, seeing there was nowhere else to go, slid down the roof on his seat. He caught the lower roof of the boiler house and banked off that to the ground, hitting hard but without damage. He picked himself up and dashed amongst some piles of lumber. He didn't hear any pursuer and after another 30 yards he stopped to catch his breath, keeping well in the shadows. After a few minutes he heard the clang of fire bells, first far away and then coming close. Addy had evidently ridden to the fire station with her bicycle.

DISTANT DAYS
Things were different when we were boys. In those distant days women were mostly angels. Nowadays women are mostly journalists, clerks, typewriters and medical students.

Muskegon Daily Chronicle

Ch   15

Petronius could hear the clanging fire wagon reach the mill, and the clamor as the fire fighters disembarked with shouts and questioning. He trotted briskly between the lumber piles. Too briskly as it turned out. In the darkness his forehead struck the end of a board, knocking him senseless for a minute. When he awoke his eyes wouldn't focus and he took a few crazy steps before sitting down sideways and vomiting on himself. He could feel blood dripping from his throbbing head. He vaguely knew he should be talking with the firefighters, telling them about the rigged boiler. But the foremost of his confused thoughts was: how could he let himself be seen this way, like a drunken, stinking derelict?

By stumbling and crawling he made his way back to his rooming house and found an empty lower bunk. He slept for a good 12 hours and awoke to find himself somewhat cleaned and bandaged, Mrs. Charlton's doing he learned.

A bit later Mrs. Charlton came and asked him if he could eat anything. She asked no further questions because Addy had filled her in on the evenings adventures. Petronius sipped a bit of soup and chewed some bread, feeling clumsy and slow, and with a still considerable ache in his head. Mrs. Charlton put a note down next to him. It was from Addy. He read: "What happened to you? Are you all right? Contact me as soon as you feel able. I'm afraid I didn't make a very convincing case by myself last night."

Sawdust Fires 97

Petronius found Addy at her typewriter in her father's office. "I took a wallop," he said by way of explanation. He eased himself into a chair and gave a brief description of his escape from the boiler room, without being specific about his blow to the head. It hurt to talk and he asked her to tell her side.

She satisfied herself he needed no further medical attention and then began her story.

A surprising number of people had already gathered, attracted by the fire bells and mill whistle. There was general confusion and milling about although Addy tried to direct the firefighter to the mill's boiler room. But without flames to address the men weren't sure how to proceed. After a few more minutes the fire chief came riding in on his horse, looking rumpled and angry. Addy heard some of the rapid exchange between the chief and his men. "No fire at all you say? Who turned in the alarm? That young lady? Not a practical joke is it? Said the boiler was going to explode?"

The chief dismounted and came over to her. "I know you. Ain't you the daughter of Terence Driscoll?"

His accusatory tone stung her. "I am."

"Does he know you've been out all by yourself in the middle of the night?"

"Mr. Bonner I'm 23 years old."

"I didn't ask that. I asked if your father knew?"

"I couldn't say. You'll have to question him." She immediately regretted her defiant answer but she felt angry as she realized her father had probably been out all night himself at the Canterbury House or some other establishment.

"I will talk to him and soon." the fire chief shot back. "Make no mistake. I don't care if you're 23 or 43. No daughter of mine would behave so. You're one of those new women ain't you? Not satisfied with a woman's share. Has to meddle in men's business. Do men's jobs. I don't agree with it."

She held her tongue.

"Now then. Tell me how you happen to be here."

She tried to steady her voice. "I was assisting a gentlemen in his investigation of an attempted arson."

"And what gentlemen would that be?"

"Mr. Jacob Larson, a detective with the fire insurance companies."

"Said he was a detective did he?"

"He is a detective."

"Then where is he now?"

"I don't know. He may be hurt."

The watchmen now pitched in with loud voices. "Weren't no detective. It were some bum. Pounded on the door and we tried to run him off. Must have been drunk or crazy."

Addy tried to make herself heard but was shouted down. "Who is she accusing us? Some street walker whore? An ugly one too."

The fire chief raised his hands in a quieting motion.

"The bum wouldn't go away," one watchman continued. "Finally broke into the boiler room through a back window. Messed with the boiler. We'll show you."

A good part of the crowd pushed in ahead of Addy and followed the fire fighters and watchmen towards the boiler room. Addy used the time to check the interior of the mill, afraid she would find Petronius lying in a heap amongst the saws. She went outside of the building, looked at the mill pond and walked between some of the piles of lumber. But it was too dark. A real search would have to wait until morning. Suddenly she felt very weary. She found her shawl and drill brace, gathered up her bicycle and pedaled home.

Petronius considered her story. "It would have helped if I'd been there to back up your side of things. Is it too late to do that now?"

Sawdust Fires 99

"Too late I'm afraid. The watchmen were questioned by the police and released this morning I understand."

"Takes care of that. Those watchmen will be gone without a trace. Just like I figured, the police, firemen and lumbermen are all in it together."

"I don't know about the police but I can't believe that's true of the fire department."

"How can you say so after your treatment last night?"

"That may have been just Chief Bonner's attitude towards me and women in general. You'll recall he testified against McClatchen at the court hearing in Grand Rapids."

"He did that."

"And furthermore I think he believed my story, because just this afternoon he announced all boilers at the sawmills would be thoroughly inspected."

"Inspected you say. That would make it harder for any mill to stage a boiler explosion I assume?"

"Yes, at least no one could blame faulty boiler equipment."

"A useful development."

"And now would be the ideal time for you to join forces with the fire department. Tell them everything about your background and activities. With their cooperation you may be able to prevent any further arson fires."

"Can't say I'm ready for that. We're doing fine on our own."

"But I may not be able to help you any more."

He looked up sharply. "Why's that?"

"Fire Chief Bonner talked with my father and now I've been given a curfew and other restrictions."

"You're going to accept that?"

"If I want to continue living at home."

"How much does your father know of my activities and your part in them?"

"I'm not sure. I didn't volunteer any information. But he

talks with lots of men all over town and may know quite a lot. He could make things hard for you. That's why you should get together with Mr. Bonner. As much as he's been unfair to me I still believe he's honest enough, or a least not in league with the arsonists."

"My experiences in Chicago don't lead me to trust city officials."

"Not every place is as bad as Chicago. You have to trust someone."

"I'll think about it some."

Petronius was thinking about such an alliance with the fire chief the next day as he headed towards Western Avenue. Just as he turned a corner he bumped into two men he recognized. But before he could react Pattone seized him in a hug, pinioning his arms and lifting him off the ground. Petronius felt the grip tighten until he couldn't breathe. Just as he was about to struggle for his life Pattone gave a shout of triumph and tossed Petronius into the air and back onto his feet. At once Shelvey rushed over, grabbed Petronius' hand and pumped it in congratulatory fashion.

"See what good friends you will be with each other?"

"Good friends. Yes, I see," Petronius muttered after taking a few seconds to recover his breath. "Well," he went on, "since we're good friends now, perhaps you'd tell me what our fight was about at the Big Deal Saloon some months back?"

Both men immediately took on contrite looks.

"That was," said Pattone, "how shall I say, a prank."

"Yes, a prank!" Shelvey repeated joyfully.

"We know you are from great Chicago, and we decided to give you our little idea of a back woodsman's joke," continued Pattone.

Petronius answered as jovially. "Just a joke. I suspected as much." Idiots! he thought to himself. Only idiots would expect him to believe such nonsense. He raised an inquiring finger. "Another question, gentlemen. Have you ever had any dealings with Angus McClatchen, the lumberman?"

The pair exchanged blank looks. "For Stratford and Hines sawmill, that is who we are working for," said Pattone. "When the logs run out for the season, soon, then we will go north to the pine woods and work for their camp."

Shelvey nodded in solemn confirmation.

"Well, that answers all my questions. You couldn't have been more helpful. I wish you good day friends." He began to move away.

"Wait!" Pattone protested. "Join us for lunch and drinks if you would possibly?"

"Very kind offer. But I have some business which won't wait."

"Our disappointment is, how shall I say, considerable," Pattone mourned.

Shelvey clasped Petronius' hand between both of his before departing.

Were they just idiots Petronius wondered to himself as he continued up the sidewalk? Or sly and dangerous conspirators? He couldn't decide. Furthermore the incident had unnerved him a good deal. Although he had kept an outward calm he felt very much flustered. The encounter reminded him of his early years at the orphanage. At 6 or 7 he was extremely small for his age, and for that reason picked on by other boys. One particular bully used to lift him up and shake him like a doll until his eyes seemed to rattle in his head, to the great amusement of the other boys. That's what the run-in with Pattone and Shelvey brought to mind. Being held up and shook, just for amusement of the town. He wondered if the lumbermen were behind it. In any case, at least for the time being, he couldn't bring himself to meet with the formidable chief Bonner.

The first weeks of November produced nothing notable except cold and dark days, with much rain and occasional sleet. All the leaves had blown off, leaving the trees grey and skeleton like. The early closing of the saw mills added to the general gloom, as the logs ran out for the season. Many of the mill workers headed north to the woods and the lumber camps, not entirely sure they'd find work there either. Quite a number decided it was time to move west.

Just before Thanksgiving Petronius received a note from Mr. Driscoll inviting him for dinner on the holiday. He assumed it was at Addy's urging.

The Thursday came and he made his way through a driving rain to the Driscoll house. It felt good to enter a warm and brightly lighted place, and smell the odors of spicy foods cooking. He was shown into a parlor by Mr. Driscoll himself and given a glass of hot cider. Sam was already there along with Joshua and Joshua's mother, the three sitting quietly in chairs. Joshua entertained himself with a book of Civil War pictures, though he looked none too happy. Petronius was introduced to another man, a Mr. Amos Burcon. He knew the name slightly. Burcon was a minor lumberman like Driscoll, though about 10 years older. And, like Driscoll, a widower.

Evidently the dinner was to be something of a showcase for Addy's new domestic skills. At least that's what Driscoll implied as he told of Addy working in the kitchen with Mrs. Fogarty since early morning.

About 1:20 they were called into the dining room. The table was full with steaming plates of food; baked goose and grouse, yams, blanched corn, buttered beans, two kinds of biscuits, baked apples and sundry small items.

After they were seated Addy read a prayer of Thanksgiving. Driscoll and Burcon listened respectfully but did not join the Amen.

After numerous favorable comments on the variety and tastiness of the food Driscoll said. "It's a grand meal that Addy has prepared for us is it not?" He seemed to direct his question mostly to Petronius.

Petronius swallowed a mouthful. "Couldn't be more delicious. Best I've eaten, I can truthfully say."

Addy spoke up in a quiet but firm voice. "I did very little really. I was in the kitchen helping, but Mrs. Fogarty directed in every way. She deserves all the credit, not me."

"Well, you're still learning Addy girl," said her father. "And I'll be seein' that you go on with your learning."

"I shall try. But I've enrolled in an artist's class as well," she said.

"You didn't ask me," he protested.

She looked unbowed. "I thought you wouldn't object."

"Art is really not a bad thing for a young lady to learn," said Burcon, pleasantly." As long as the domestic skills aren't neglected, to be sure." The words seemed to soothe Driscoll.

The conversation returned to the food and the general unpleasantness of the weather. Petronius noticed Joshua eating well while maintaining an angry, pouting look.

As they were finishing the pie Driscoll and Burcon began discussing the merits of the various western forests and their potential for sizeable profits. The hauling and sawing of types of logs was gone into in some detail.

"It will be a grand business to be sure," said Burcon, summing up. "Whether we cut redwood, or fir, or pine, it's all important work we'll be about, as well as making money. Clearing the forests so the country can build and move ahead."

"Important work indeed." Driscoll agreed. "We'll be providing the land people need for agriculture and towns and industry."

Sam could contain himself no longer and slapped his hand down on the table. "It is wrong to clear so much of the forests. Where will the birds and animals live? They need a place. The animals and birds are God's creatures as well. Is what I say not true?"

Burcon gave a short laugh. "I thought this fellow worked for you Driscoll?"

Driscoll reddened a bit. "He does. Though perhaps not much longer."

Addy jumped in quickly. "Sam is absolutely right. Both of you would do well to listen to what he says."

Sam, encouraged, went on. "The white man could learn much from the ways of the Indians, just as we Indians are expected to learn from the white man."

"The ways of the Indians are long past," said Burcon dismissively. "New and progressive philosophies are taking hold. It's in the very nature of things. Furthermore, it's been given to us, the white man, to rule. And rule not just in this country, to be sure, but in the other lands as well."

"Addy replied hotly. "I can't believe God wants one race to be lord and master over all the world's peoples. That was not the message Jesus delivered at all."

Burcon had reached the end of his patience. "Young lady, in my day daughters held their tongues and deferred to their fathers and their elders. As should you."

"In some things I can," she said. "But not in this."

"Play some music!" Driscoll commanded. He got to his feet. "Be playin' something on the piano."

All moved into the parlor. Addy brought out some sheet music and began to play softly on the small instrument.

As a louder piece was being played, Driscoll leaned over to Petronius and said in an offhand way, "Would you be willing to do some private work for me as a detective?"

"Of what nature?"

"We can discuss the details some time at my office should you be interested."

Petronius was always looking for ways to supplement his income and so he nodded his interest. He suspected Driscoll still considered him a hopeful match for Addy, and this was one more thing to move the process along.

Though the sweet tones of the music brought a measure of calm to all present, an air of dispute still lingered and the party broke up sooner than it might have otherwise.

A cold rain continued to fall as Petronius made his way back to his rooming house.

SOCIAL SUCCESS

The girl who aspires to social success and fashion must buckle on her armor. If she shows a fractious or peremptory irritability in small things, if she is fussy about her supposed rights, if she keeps people waiting, if she is not polite, or if she is too polite, she will not be popular.

Muskegon Daily Chronicle

Ch 16

The first day of December brought a cheering snow fall; six inches of white frosting to decorate the trees and buildings and cover the grey landscape. The newspaper used the term "good slipping" to describe the conditions of the streets, and many people got out their sleighs and winter harness and rode about town for the sheer pleasure of it.

Petronius too was cheered by the change in weather and he looked through the newspaper for ideas to celebrate this beginning of winter. He saw another mention of the upcoming annual Christmas Charity Ball. The affair had been touted for weeks, both in ads and newspaper articles. The Ball was to be held earlier than usual, the first Saturday in December this year. But early or not the cream of society would surely be there, so said the stories, because Muskegon's elite could always be counted on to support right causes. By all accounts the Ball Committee had outdone itself, soaring to new heights of imagination in planning the evening's program and decorations. Tickets sold for the substantial price of $25 per couple but the proceeds would go to a most worthy charity, the Home for the Friendless.

Petronius made up his mind to go. If he was to be a rich and powerful man some day it would be advantageous to learn how the cream of society conducted itself. Also, to have some social graces would help when it came time to attract a beautiful woman to his side. He could use a few extras, such as elegant manners, to balance the diminishment of his physical appearance.

He would invite Addy to go with him of course. She wouldn't exactly be the prize escort. But then he didn't have a lot of choices. And he wasn't intending to impress anyone this time. It would be sort of an exercise, a practice for the real thing some distance in the future.

As he expected, Addy accepted his invitation to the Ball, even though the time was quite short, as she said. Other women apparently had already spent a month planning their gowns and accessories. He quizzed her on his own attire, and she gave him a list of the proper clothes to rent.

The evening of the Ball came and Petronius arrived at the Driscoll house right on time and outfitted in his formal suit with tails, boiled shirt, black tie, patent leather shoes and white gloves. He cut a rather bold figure he thought. Of course with all the other gentlemen similarly attired he wouldn't particularly stand out, yet he felt more fashionable than ever before.

Addy was equally prompt, as she came down directly after Mrs. Fogarty's call. She had obviously made her own gown. It lacked the finished look of store merchandise. Yet it fit her lean figure well enough and had a certain richness, the material being a dark green with strands of muted red, yellow and blue woven through it. Her hair had been carefully wound into something she called Empire Style. There was no helping her face, of course, although it had been softened by an application of facial creme of some sort. Her father was there and added some admiring words before sending them on their way.

The evening air was cold and crisp but without wind, and they decided to dismiss the cab he had waiting and walk to the Occidental Hotel. A few small piles of frozen snow remained on the sidewalks and they stepped carefully around them in their delicate shoes.

"Are you a good dancer?" she asked.

"I've never danced. Never been to a ball either."

"Oh my!" she said in surprise. "In a way I'm glad to hear that. I was afraid I might embarrass you with my dancing. But what will we do if we don't dance? Just sit and watch?"

"No, we'll dance. I'll watch how the others do it and copy their steps. It can't be so hard to learn."

"Well it's a little harder than that I think."

"You've danced a bit then?"

"I took a some dancing lessons as a girl. I might have taken more if the classes had been limited to girls. But we were required to pair up with boys and the ones matched with me howled in protest and pretended such anguish I couldn't continue."

"Pretty hard for a young girl I expect."

"Until those boys in the dancing class described me as ugly I had never thought of myself that way. I knew I wasn't pretty but my playmates growing up treated me fairly, at least no differently than an average child."

Petronius tried to be sympathetic. "Can't say I was ever called ugly, but I was small and picked on a lot as a boy. Real shy and quiet I was. Didn't do well in school at first."

"Did you ever know anything of your parents?"

"Never was told anything and didn't care to ask. The toughest boys made believe they'd kind of sprung to life by themselves without parents. And I tried to imitate the toughest boys."

"Did imitating help?"

"Not much. Still got picked on. It was only through athletics I gained my confidence. I have old Father Brubacher to thank for that. He coached me and encouraged me. Taught me boxing and coached me in baseball. Used to play catch with me and pitch me batting practice hours at a time. In fact it was for him I went to the seminary, even though I knew I wasn't well suited for it. Speaking of coaching, I'll need some coaching on a few things. Having been brought up in an orphanage, and then only working with men in sports and the police force, I haven't been to many social soirees. You'll have to help me with some of the niceties."

"I haven't attended many soirees myself you know. However if you'll agree to be the dance instructor I'll coach all the rest."

A jam of traffic pressed around the entrance of the hotel as most of the evenings participants arrived by carriage, choosing to save their exertions for the dance floor. Petronius and Addy could feel the air of festivity as they joined the flow of ball goers.

Electric lights in the hotel lobby had been extinguished in favor of sparse candles, making the entree into the brilliantly lighted ballroom all the more dramatic. The four corners of that large space had been filled with pine boughs, and those woven together to form many small alcoves. Nesting in the alcoves were stuffed birds in colorful variety; partridge, quail, grouse, passenger pigeon and others. The pine bough theme was continued at other strategic places in the room, with the dark green of the branches offset with many red ribbons tied and bunched to look like chrysanthemums. A large fir tree, laden with electrically lit artificial candles, filled the very center of the room. A dozen musicians, now at leisure, but equipped with a variety of stringed instruments, formed a circle about the tree.

The refreshment tables had already been laid out and shone as colorful as any of the decorations. Beds of lettuce and cracked ice held oysters, crab meat, smoked salmon and other delectables. Bottles of wine stood guard at the corners in uniforms of ribbon and foil.

As the couples entered the room they couldn't help but take deep breaths to catch the scent of pine and perfumed candles. Then they toured the room to savor the decorations and to examine, without being obvious, the attire of other ladies. Many of the outfits shimmered with obvious expense. More than a few suffered from an excess of necklaces, bracelets and brooches.

Petronius and Addy promenaded about the room along with the other couples. "When I was growing up," she said, "my girlfriends and I dreamed over and over of going to the Charity Ball. We planned our dresses and our hair and our dance cards. I'd almost come to think I'd never get to one except by serving on one of the committees."

"And now that you're here, what do you think?"

"The fanciness of it disturbs me a little. Why do we have to be bribed by so much opulence to contribute to a good cause? I should think a simpler affair would net more money. But all the same I find the whole of it lovely, and wouldn't have missed being here."

As the orchestra began tuning up she said, "Shall we sit and observe for a while?"

"We'll observe better if we get out among the others." He pulled her out onto the center of the floor. "What's the first dance?"

She checked her program. "Strauss waltz. I may be able to help us through this. The waltz was taught in the classes I attended."

She took his good left hand with her right and draped her other hand over his right shoulder. As they moved she counted out the rhythm. "ONE, two, three. ONE, two, three." He stepped stiffly at first, but gradually relaxed and was able to feel his motions more in time with the music. By the end they were gliding about in a reasonable approximation of dancers.

"You do learn fast," said Addy.

"A bit like athletics it is," he replied.

"Polka next," she said. "And time for me to turn over

coaching duties to you."

They more or less stumbled through the polka, not ever quite catching up to the faster pace of the music. But Petronius was not discouraged and they pressed on, dance after dance, through quadrilles and lanciers. Petronius knew they made a strange looking couple. Addy, even in her low slippers, was the tallest woman on the floor. He noticed other couples staring at them, and at times whispering jokes as well.

"Doesn't seem to bother you much when people laugh" he commented to Addy.

"It does some, but I've gotten used to it. And growing up a pariah does have advantages. I've learned people's opinions aren't nearly as important as I once thought, so I go my own way. Also, it's helped me to develop sympathy with other outcasts, especially the Indians."

At times their missteps were comical, and they enjoyed those almost as much as their successes. One time Addy tripped over Petronius' wrongly placed foot and he caught her about the waist with his good arm and held on for a bit, feeling her taut stomach.

As the evening wore on their performance on the floor improved markedly. Petronius surprised even himself with his ability to learn the dances. Not just that he was physically able to do the steps but that he seemed to have the proper ear for the cadences of the music and how the motions flowed with them. And he was somehow able to instruct Addy as well.

She in turned coached him in what a refined gentleman would do in all the particulars of the occasion; how to accompany a lady to and from the dance floor, how to bow, and how to secure refreshments and consume them gracefully. He was glad to have the instruction.

At his asking Addy pointed out some of the wealthier couples, including Mr. and Mrs. Martin Crisp, the J. J. Talmans, and the Detwilers. McClatchen was not in attendance but it was announced he had sent a check for $200 to be added to the proceeds; that news bringing hardy applause.

As the evening grew late many of the gentlemen began cutting in on certain ladies. Mrs. Talman proved to be a favorite. Quite a bit younger than her lumberman husband, she combined beauty with elegance of dress. Plus she had a way of leaning back and bursting out with great laughter at any witticism from her partner.

At one o'clock an extra surprise was announced by members of the planning committee. New snow had fallen and a fleet of large sleighs had been arranged and now awaited for any who wished transportation home.

Each sleigh held six couples and they exchanged shouts with the other conveyances like school children as they slid off into the night. Snow flakes continued to sweep down, misting everything with a pleasing gauze. Even the weather had been arranged by the planning committee, everyone in Petronius' sleigh agreed. The driver inquired as to whose residence lay nearest but no one wanted the ride to end quickly so false addresses were given. The man handled the jokes with good nature and seemed to enjoy the extra riding as much as any. The cold night air brought a glow to everyone's face and they sang songs. Eventually they tired.

The sleigh waited as Petronius escorted Addy to the door of her house. A lamp burned but no one seemed about. She fixed him with a wide smile, a look of adulation almost.

"This has been a wonderful evening for me. I hope it has for you as well."

"Indeed. Most enjoyable." He took her hand and rather clumsily kissed it.

She laughed. "You'll need a bit more practice if you're to become a real dandy."

For several evenings after that, as he lay in his bunk preparing for sleep he thought of his success the night of the

Charity Ball. He had been graceful and witty, and had charmed Addy down to her toes. Of course he was likely the first man to pay any real attention to her, even though that interest was mostly feigned. He especially recalled the look she had given him at her front door. He was sure at that moment, if he'd asked, she would have let him into the house and allowed him to share her bed. It was a powerful feeling knowing he could have his way with her if he chose. Not that Addy's conquest would be considered much of a prize in bragging circles. Still there was a certain pleasure in knowing he could humble her, bring her down a notch; Miss ever so gracious, Miss know everything, Miss holier than thou Addy Driscoll.

NO QUIETUDE

Sitting Bull, the Sioux chief, was shot and killed at his camp here early Monday morning by the Indian police while resisting arrest. The arrest of Sitting Bull had been ordered by the War Department four or five days ago as it became evident that, while he was permitted to run around corrupting the weak minds of his tribe, there could be no quietude.

Muskegon Daily Chronicle

Ch 17

Addy found Petronius at an early card game in one of the saloons. She insisted he step out for a talk.

"Sam is in the hospital. He was hit last evening by a streetcar."

"How badly hurt?"

"They don't know yet. He was unconscious last night."

"How did he happen to tangle with a streetcar?"

"One of the hospital staff said they smelled alcohol on his clothing and think he might have been drunk."

"Didn't think Sam was a drinking man."

"He's not. The police were notified and they questioned some of the proprietors of the drinking establishments. Sam was seen in the company of your former acquaintances, Pattone and his friend."

"Aha! With those two involved there's got to be more to the story."

"That's why I wanted you to go with me this morning, in case Sam is able to talk."

When they got to the hospital they found Sam sitting up in bed. A considerable bruise discolored the side of his face and a gash parted his scalp. Apparently nothing major had been broken other than a pair of ribs. In fact he would be allowed to leave the hospital that very day.

After greeting Addy and Petronius with a rueful grin he complained, "bad headache."

"I know." Addy patted his hand and looked for a minute as if she would cry, but smiled through it. "If you feel able, Sam, tell us what happened."

Sam asked for a glass of water and began his story in a slow laconic voice.

He was in town alone, to do some Christmas shopping for Joshua and his daughter, visiting the stores on Western Ave. The shopping wasn't going all that well but he enjoyed looking in the bright shop windows with their displays and decorations.

He was walking past the Steindler House on Western when two men came out and hailed him.

"Mr. Washoo, favor us for a few minutes would you please?" the big one called.

"Yes, we desire to hire your services," added the other.

"What services?" he answered back.

"Fishing guide, and hunting too. But mostly fishing."

"I do some. Not in the winter."

"Fine, fine, let's talk where it's warm." They guided him inside and to a small table near the front window. He recognized the bigger man as Pattone. The smaller one he had seen too, but didn't know his name. The small fellow introduced himself and then sat smiling broadly while Pattone went to secure drinks and lunch from the bar.

Sam didn't mind the food. He would eat as much they could bring. But he made it clear he would accept no more than one glass of beer.

"Entirely as you wish. You are the guest," said Pattone as he set down sandwiches.

"What kind of fishing do you men prefer?" Sam asked.

Sawdust Fires 116

They looked at each other in puzzlement for a second before Pattone said, "All kinds of fishing. You may choose for us. That's why we wish to hire you."

"Yes," Shelvay added. "We like to fish."

"You have fish poles?"

"No. We would, how shall I say, need to take loan of those."

"You like to fish but have no fish poles?"

"We like to fish but we've been very busy," protested Shelvay

"We work at the saw mill," said Pattone.

"I'm busy too," Sam answered back. He realized he was being made a joke. Still, he could enjoy a joke, even if he was the center of it, as long as it stayed a joke.

"We know you are busy, Mr. Washoo," soothed Pattone. "That's why we come to you so soon. We wish to hire you before all the others hire you and you become, how shall I say, booked up. We know you are the best fishing guide in town and a great woodsman." Pattone moved another glass towards Sam. "If you please, tell us a story of a big fish you've caught."

Sam pushed the new drink away and continued to sip slowly from his original glass. So, okay he would joke with them. He told of how he had caught a 25 pound pike in Muskegon Lake, making it a fish story, having the pike jump into and out of the boat, each time snagging a piece of clothing as it went. The two seemed to enjoy the serious way he related the details.

When the story was finished Pattone slapped him on the back in appreciation.

"Yes, that's the kind of fishing we want to do," Shelvay enthused.

As Sam began another story Pattone pushed a glass quickly towards Sam, this time spilling some of the liquid on his clothes. The pair apologized and dabbed at the wet spots,

Sawdust Fires 117

but Sam saw the spill as deliberate.

He got to his feet. "I must go now. You gentlemen are to be thanked for the refreshment. We will get together some future time for fishing."

"No, the thanks are all to you, Mr. Washoo, for your time and understanding."

They made no attempt to stop him as made his way out. He felt some relief as he got onto the sidewalk. But in no time the pair came running out after him.

"Wait, you forgot to tell us when the fishing season begins," yelled Shelvay.

"Not for many months. Now good night. I wish to go my own way."

But the two were on each side of him, one taking his shoulders and the other with an arm about the waist, as if guiding and supporting a drunken man. Soon they stepped over the curb and into the street, walking along with the carriage traffic.

"I no longer wish to be part of your joke," Sam yelled, trying to throw off their arms.

But they began singing loudly, French songs, like they were a merry trio having a riotous evening together. The louder he protested the more boisterously they sang.

As they continued east on Western Avenue, Sam could see the headlight and hear the rumble of the approaching street railway. He made up his mind to break free. But just as he twisted away they ran forward and pushed him hard into the path of the oncoming streetcar. He
felt he had upset their timing somewhat but still he couldn't avoid the collision and in an instant received a tremendous jolt amidst a bright light which quickly dimmed.

"An inept pair, those two," commented Petronius as Sam ended his story. "But dangerous enough. They meant to have you look like a drunk who'd wandered onto the tracks."

Addy had a serious look on her face and said, "We need to find the reason behind this."

"Well," said Petronius, "we're being sent a strong message. Don't know who's sending it but I mean to get some answers from Pattone and Shelvay, if they haven't left town."

Addy accompanied him down the hall. She would stay on for a bit to arrange for Sam's release and to have the bills sent to her father. She took a strong hold on his sleeve. "I want you to promise me you'll act with caution."

"I won't do anything foolish but I'll do what's necessary."

She seemed angry with his answer but let him go.

Petronius first went to the bank and got his pistol and cartridges. Then he proceeded to the Stratford & Hines mill where the pair worked as lumber pilers. He wasn't surprised to find they hadn't reported for work that day. A check of their rooming house gave every indication the pair had departed during the night. He questioned the ticket man and freight handlers at the railway station but no one had seen the fugitives.

By then time Petronius was accompanied by not one but two shadowers, and both tough looking gents. They made no secret of their job either. He thought of confronting them with his revolver and demanding an explanation. He came close to doing it but recalled Addy's caution. The men might very well have revolvers of their own.

When he reported his lack of accomplishment to Addy she flared up. "I think it's time you went to the authorities with your identity, background and entire business."

He answered in as strong a tone. "Are you saying my methods caused the attack on Sam?"

She took a deep breath and softened her voice. "Sam was almost killed last night and I'm quite upset. But I don't blame you for what happened. I just feel we can't delay getting to the reason. What is your theory on all this?"

"I can only say more of the same, the lumbermen trying

to scare me off the arsonists."

"You've said in the past the surveillance and actions against you were out of proportion to any threat you posed. Doesn't the attack on Sam seem equally strange?"

"So it does."

"And even if you were to be scared off, wouldn't the insurance companies send another detective?"

"Very likely."

"Then what would the arsonists gain?"

"Can't say."

"So will you do as I've suggested, talk to the police and whoever else?"

"I can. Not sure that will unravel things for us."

"It may not, but it could clarify what were dealing with, an arson investigation alone or something more."

He had to admit her assessment made sense and he had no better plan of his own. Still he felt a bit resentful at being told his business.

The truth was, Petronius didn't trust the police, not after what had happened in Chicago. But he marched himself to the police station in the City Hall building. There he filed a formal complaint regarding the attack on Sam. The policeman he talked with was a sergeant and exhibited, if not hostility, as least disdain towards his interviewee.

The man set down his pencil and announced, "We'll handle things from this point, sir."

Petronius then went into his own background and activities and insisted those particulars be written down also. The sergeant grudgingly picked up his pencil and did so.

"And what are we to do with this personal account of yours, sir?"

"Why, report it to your chief, man!" Petronius snapped. He wanted to add, "and to whichever of the big lumbermen you care to."

The sergeant put a decisive check on the corner of the

sheet. "Marked for his immediate attention, sir. Anything else?"

Petronius told of the numerous surveillances he had been subjected to and suggested those needed looking into.

"Were you assaulted on any of those occasions, sir?"

He hadn't been.

"Threatened at all?"

Again no.

The man couldn't keep from smiling. "I would think an experienced detective from Chicago would be prepared to deal with some, shall we say, small matters with his own resources. Not that official assistance isn't offered when time avails. We search for lost kittens and puppies too when time avails."

Petronius tried to match the deprecating tone of his adversary. "When the force has time, sergeant, I suggest it track down Pattone and Shelvay. Finding two near murderers should be worth the efforts of even some of your best men." The two exchanged curt nods and Petronius took his leave.

While he was stirred up he vowed to see the big man himself. He wasn't sure what he'd say other than repeat his report to the police. But when he tried to make an appointment to see McClatchen he was told the lumberman was preparing to leave for Washington State, and couldn't be diverted. He was expected to return sometime in February.

Petronius didn't go into all the painful details when he reported on his mission to Addy. In any case her mind was on another problem.

"The attack on Sam has Joshua all riled up. He wants to fight everybody. Sam would like me to talk with him. I'm not sure I know how to handle this."

"Don't look at me to help. I'd probably go along with all Joshua's thoughts of retribution. What's Sam been telling the boy?"

"The same as what I would say. The Lord commands us to return good for evil. But Joshua sees the attempt on his

Sawdust Fires 121

grandfather as another attack on Indians. And coming right after the death of Chief Sitting Bull it's all the harder to take."

"The newspaper report says Sitting Bull was killed by some of his own people, tribal police officers."

"But ordered by white authorities. In any case Sitting Bull has become a symbol of defiance for all Indians, especially after the Ghost Dance troubles of last year."

"I've heard of this Ghost Dance, but don't know what it's about."

"According to Sam the dance enlists the spirits of dead ancestors in driving the white people from Indian lands. The government sees it as an effort to stir up another Indian war."

"So all this has gotten Joshua on the warpath has it? What's he plan to do exactly?"

"I don't know. I don't think he knows himself."

"Tell Sam to keep Joshua from getting his hands on any guns."

"I'm sure he knows that already."

"Then I don't have much else to offer."

She thought for a few moments. "Perhaps Joshua would like to see the stores in Chicago, decorated for Christmas. I could take him on the train."

"Any kid would like that."

The Chicago plan was put into action with salutary results. The fire in Joshua cooled to embers, and Christmas in Muskegon passed peacefully. There followed a series of snowstorms which buried the community through much of the winter.

CULTIVATED TASTE

Talking about artists in Muskegon, a glimpse in any of the framers shops will reveal works of theirs not to be ashamed of. There are a number of ladies here who do considerable work in oil, and, though, mostly from copy, do it in a manner that shows cultivated taste.

Muskegon Daily Chronicle

Ch 18

Towards April, Addy visited Petronius at his rooming house. "I have a great favor to ask of you." she said. "My art instruction has reached the point where we're drawing human faces. I need someone to sit for me. Would you be my subject?"

"You mean paint a portrait of me?"

"Not a portrait. Just a pencil sketch really, and it won't take more than an hour."

"How about your father? Wouldn't he be willing to do it?"

"He considers my art frivolous, and does as little as possible to encourage it."

"Then I don't know if I should encourage it either," he said. She gave him a wry look. After a suitable pause he said, "Yes, I'll do it. You've done a great deal for me and my work."

He showed up at her house late the next afternoon in his best suit and clean shirt. She had set up her drawing stand in the sitting room and positioned a chair for him which caught the rays of the afternoon sun. A draped cloth provided a backdrop. He took his place with some awkwardness. He wondered for a time what to do with his bad arm and finally grasped it with his good hand in what seemed a manly pose. She ordered several changes in his posture before they could begin.

"Am I allowed to talk or do you want a stone expression?"

"It doesn't matter while I'm roughing in the first outlines. I'll tell you when it's time to hold your head perfectly still."

"You said you took up this art stuff to make a history of the lumber business?

"That's been my intention. But I have to admit photographs would do a better job than my sketches. But I continue, partly for vanity I suppose, to see myself as more cultured than the average person."

"I'm sure it does give you some smack of culture. More than your tree climbing. How did you come to favor climbing trees?"

"It's something I always did as a child. I keep on with it because it gives me a feeling of peace. Also it reminds me of a very special moment I had once."

"What was that?"

"One summer evening I climbed a tree near Lake Michigan and when I reached the top and looked out I was struck by just an incredible sense of joy and beauty. The feeling just surpassed all words to describe it. It lasted only a second but I've never forgotten it. Now, hold still and don't talk."

Petronius kept quiet for almost a minute but then couldn't resist answering. "That's most interesting. Myself, I had a dream several times when I was a boy which gave me special feelings. I'm sitting in a shady pavilion watching a baseball game on a bright sunny day. I'm filled with what you might call perfect happiness, but a lot more than that too. Like you, I haven't got quite the proper words."

She set down her pencil. "I wonder if many people haven't felt the same thing but never told anyone. I once asked my father if he had. "

"What'd he say?"

"He said if he had it was long forgotten, and best so, like

the thoughts of a child."

"I haven't had those dreams for many years but I haven't forgotten them. I've often made special trips to look at ballparks, though I can't say any of 'em ever came close to my dream."

"It must be the way heaven feels like, what we experienced. Perhaps we're each given a taste of heaven so we know it's real."

She took up her pencil and they continued, mostly in silence.

"You can look now."

He got up and went around to view the sketch and then voiced his approval. "I have to say I wasn't expecting much of a masterpiece, but this has turned out fine." The picture showed a fairly good likeness, in fact made him more distinguished than he deserved. Not only that, she had sketched him in a baseball jersey.

"Thank you," she answered with some pride. "I've practiced quite a bit with my own face and a mirror."

"Oh? I'd like to see those."

"Most have been thrown away."

"I'll look at what's left," he insisted.

She reluctantly pulled down a large folder from a wall shelf and drew out three pencil portraits of herself, one from straight on and two from the sides.

"These are fairly good."

"I do have some talent with faces I think. I'm what's called a good copyist. But the ones you see here are the best of many tries." She began to put away the folder but another item she had skipped over caught Petronius' eye.

"Hold on. What's this?" He took the folder and pulled out a sketch which showed a clear, well-shaped face. "Is this meant to be you?"

"She colored in embarrassment and said, "I imagined myself without scars and used a picture of my mother as an aid."

He frankly enjoyed her discomfort but said only, "Well, your mother must have been a handsome woman."

"Oh, I almost forgot," she snatched the sketch back and quickly put the folder away. "We have a business matter to discuss. Just this afternoon I received a most interesting letter from Mr. Wanagan. Do you remember him riding with us on the train up to the lumber camp?"

"He was the timber looker with the damaged leg?"

"Correct. He's a shacker now in the Upper Peninsula, cutting railroad ties and fence posts. He claims to have located one of McClatchen's missing night watchmen."

"Oh? How?"

"He doesn't say.

She handed him the piece of rough note paper. The letter was written in a large but neat hand by pencil:

To Miss Adelaide Driscoll

I write to you now because you was kind to me in the past. I seek advice about the men who was night watchmen for McClatchen. The ones the big reward was advertised for. I believe I know the whereabouts of one. I could not very well bring the man down there by myself but with some help it could be done. I would share the reward for the help. Another idea is to write directly to Mr. McClatchen telling the whereabouts of the man. That would not get me the full reward maybe but would be easier for me. What do you think of the idea? The reward money would be pretty useful to me in my old age. I await your reply in due time.

Orville Wanagan.

Petronius noted the St. Ignace post office address printed at the bottom of the page. "Do you think he could be right about this?"

"East-West Wanagan is as methodical and reliable a

witness as you'll ever see, and if he says he's found the watchman I believe it."

Petronius put the letter down and thought for a minute. "Well then, I'm the man to help Wanagan. I could use part of that reward money. I'll travel to St. Ignace myself. But when you write to Wanagan tell him not to let the news out. The last thing we want is McClatchen learning about it and overturning our efforts."

Addy immediately got out a sheet of notepaper and began an answering letter.

The more Petronius considered the turn of events the more pleased he became. "This will help in every way possible," he crowed. "The insurance companies will be relieved from paying for the fire, and with the biggest man in town brought to court for arson the other lumbermen aren't likely to try any new fires. Besides, we'll be collecting reward money right out McClatchen's pocket. That'll be a sight to see, McClatchen paying for his own arson witness."

Addy sounded more cautious. "You've got to get the man safely back here and hear what he says before any of that can happen."

"You're right there. We'll have to keep it secret. It'll take some planning. My movements are still being watched on occasion. After you finish your letter maybe we could get out your maps and consider routes and times."

Petronius left a week later. He had collected his revolver and a pair of wrist manacles and packed them in a small traveling bag along with a change of clothes. For the first leg of his journey, he took the train east all the way to Lansing. There he detrained and waited on the station platform for some time, reading a copy of Sporting Life. He had hoped to slip unnoticed onto the train for Howard City, which angled to the northwest. But a fellow traveler also waited, and watched him, and was obvious enough about it too. The man had the physique and demeanor of one not easily put off his purpose.

Sawdust Fires 127

The Detroit train came and went. Petronius waited until the Howard City train was pulling out before snatching up his bag. It took all of his considerable running ability to reach the departing passenger car, but he managed to fling himself up and onto the steps. His pursuer also made the dash but lacked the required foot speed. Petronius felt sure the man would wire ahead for someone to meet the train in Howard City, but he had a plan to deal with that as well.

He had thought about packing a disguise but considered disguises rather silly. Moreover his bad arm made any disguise difficult.

His plan was simple enough. When the train got close to Howard City he jumped off the moving car. He skinned himself a bit in the landing, but recovered and hiked into some nearby woods. There he gathered himself a pile of dried leaves and camped overnight, not comfortably but tolerably.

The next morning he walked ahead to the station in time to catch the train for Petosky and Mackinaw City. As he settled himself in his seat he observed his fellow passengers, none of whom appeared to have the slightest interest in him. He had shaken off his pursuit. It confirmed that he indeed did have aptitude as a detective.

He felt only optimism for the trip ahead. The planned task seemed well within his abilities. And when he returned with the watchman in hand it would be judged a sizeable coup. The reward money would go towards building up his capital as well, for his future assault on the Chicago big men. He was hungry now, not having had a good meal for some time, but he could hold out until Mackinaw City. He pulled out a small book he had borrowed from the library. It was a mystery involving a French detective, written by Edgar Allan Poe.

Sawdust Fires   128

Petronius Frisk, as sketched by Addy Driscoll

Addy Driscoll's idealized face, as drawn by herself

PERFECT YOUTH
Once more life's perfect youth will all come back
And for a moment there
I shall stand fresh and fair
And drop the garment care
Once more my perfect youth will nothing lack.

Muskegon Daily Chronicle

Ch 19

The trip across the Mackinac Straits by ferry proved a bumpy one, and if it had lasted longer Petronius might have gone down seasick. But he felt chipper as he set foot on the St. Ignace side. Wanagan's last letter had said he would meet Petronius at the dock, or otherwise be found in the Red Pine Saloon. Petronius went in search of that establishment.

He found the rough looking timber cruiser sitting at a table and in a cordial mood, whether from the liquid just consumed or the promise of reward money.

"How did you come to find the man," asked Petronius as they left the saloon and went about renting horses and getting a few provisions.

"Got friends among the Ottawa Indians. They know all that goes in and out of the woods. Said there was another old grizzler like me 50 mile northwest of here cutting posts and ties. I traveled up there to take a look."

"You're sure he's one of the watchmen are you?"

"Elisha Bennett. I seed his picture before I left Muskegon. I got a memory only needs look at things once. Just like I can go through a woods and always remember my directions."

The forests of the Upper Peninsula had a wilder feel than the woods Petronius had tromped through with Addy. These woods held more cedars, more hemlocks, more firs and more swamps. There were few trails to follow and those proved tough going for horses and men.

"Good thing for you it ain't bug time yet," rasped Wanagan. "I'm toughened to 'em, but with you they'd have a high old time."

They camped overnight just short of the spot and then came onto the clearing early the next morning. The sun had barely begun to filter through the trees highlighting some piles of cedar ties and poles surrounding a tiny shack.

"He may be alerted," said Wanagan as they crept close.

Petronius shoved open the door with his shoulder, pistol in hand. Five feet away stood the man in long underwear and brandishing a stick of firewood. "What be the meaning of this?" he menaced, shaking the stick.

"Steady on and I'll explain our business. If you would, toss your stick back under the stove," suggested Petronius in a calm voice.

The man sized up Petronius for another 30 seconds and then discarded the piece of firewood. Petronius put his revolver in his pocket and motioned Wanagan inside. "Is this man Elisha Bennett?"

Wanagan nodded in the affirmative.

"My name's Edward Brown," the man protested. "Who's he anyway to say I'm Bennett?"

"My companion here is Orville Wanagan."

"Wanagan, I've heard of a Wanagan, but he don't know me, otherwise he'd say I'm Brown. Now on what account are you looking for this Bennett?" The man had a high pitched, rapid fire voice.

"The man were looking for was a watchman the night McClatchen's mill burned. We mean to return him to the court in Grand Rapids. There's a sizable reward"

"That's well intended enough but I'm afraid I can't help in positive way. Don't know a Bennett myself."

Petronius handed the wrist manacles to Wanagan. "Put these on him."

"Hold on! You want to haul me all the way to Grand Rapids? What if you got the wrong man?"

"We'll have wasted considerable effort true enough. Now, what in the way of clothing and other articles will you be taking along? We have a horse waiting."

When Bennett tired of further protest, he put on a pair of pants, then took a burlap sack and selected a few items. Petronius used the time to look around. The shack held only a stove, a chair, and a bunk. Some canned goods rested on a rough shelf. The place smelled of spoiled food and unwashed clothes.

They got Bennett mounted and going down the trail with Wanagan in the lead and Petronius following. The man's face took on a tragic look. It was a poor face to begin with, narrow and pinched, with a light beard and blue veins showing. They had gone about ten miles when Bennett spoke up.

"I'll make you gentlemen a deal. I'll tell every last detail of what happened for certain considerations."

"That's of no use to us," replied Petronius "The reward is for your return to the court. The court's the one interested in hearing details."

"I haven't anything else to offer. Got no cash."

Petronius made no answer and they rode another 10 miles in silence.

"Well," Bennett started in again. "I'll tell it to you anyway. I admit I and my partner, we started the fire. But not for who you might think. It wasn't McClatchen's doing at all. Another fella, a lumberman named Driscoll set us to it and paid us."

"Terence Driscoll?" Petronius yelled ahead to the man.

"That's the man. It was done to settle accounts between him and McClatchen. The way Driscoll had it figured, McClatchen would lose the insurance money for his mill and get charged with arson besides. We were instructed to make it look not real suspicious but similar to the Michigan Shingle and Lumber fire."

Petronius groaned inwardly. After a short time they stopped, dismounted and sat on the ground to share some cans of beans and water. Wanagan's face had taken on a worried look.

Bennett continued his story as he ate, addressing himself to Petronius. "At two in the morning we gathered up some sawdust and edgings and tossed a match to 'em. Simple. Didn't use any kerosene. Then we pulled the emergency hose out and got her tangled around as if we had tried to quench the flames. When the fire got along far enough we turned in the alarm. We told the firemen it was a hot bearing which smouldered and ignited the sawdust. Later, in all the excitement, we slipped away."

"What did Driscoll pay you?" growled Petronius.

"A thousand each. A thousand, and told us to get ourselves far away to where we'd never be found."

"Then how did you come to be at that shack up there?" Petronius shot back.

"That's a sad story that is. I made a mistake by not resisting the urge to spend a little of the money. I laid over a night in Chicago to sample some of the frolic a big city can offer. Are either of you gentlemen familiar with Halsted Street?"

"I'm from Chicago," Petronius answered curtly.

"If I were to do it over I'd fly like an arrow, like my partner done."

"Where's he now?"

"Mexico I think. Anyways at one of the establishments on Halsted Street I got dosed with bad whiskey, got beat up, got my money taken. I didn't dare go to the police for fear they'd hold me and send me back to Muskegon. Had no choice but go back to the woods. I'm familiar with these woods up here. Roamed 'em when I was a youngster. But if I had the chance now I'd go right over into Canada."

They mounted up and started off again. Bennett continued to talk. "You may as well take your revolver and put a bullet in me right now. That's what my life'll be worth if you get me to Grand Rapids. I'll have McClatchen ready to hang me for disloyalty and Driscoll at my throat for fouling up his plans. Hard to say which one will be the more dangerous."

"You are in a fix aren't you?" Petronius confirmed. But he was thinking about his own plans and what to do about them. After a few more miles Petronius called ahead to Wanagan. "We'll change course and head to your shack."

"Why?" croaked Wanagan in protest as much as question.

"Tell you when we get there." He wouldn't say more.

When Bennett saw his story was having some effect on events he brightened and became positively convivial. He asked the full names of his traveling companions. He pointed out the the heads of ferns poking through the pine needles and old leaves as signs of the coming Spring. He explained his qualifications and desirability as a night watchmen. "Men liked to have me as a partner," he said "I kept 'em awake with my interesting talks. I'm a gabber I am."

At their next sit down, Bennett turned his attention to Wanagan. "Orville Wanagan. Sure. East-West Wanagan. Sure, I remember now. Didn't you work for years as timber looker for Talman?"

Wanagan grunted.

"You should be living in a fine house yourself after all the prime tracts you staked out. But no, you got a shack in the woods like me." He shook his head in disbelief. "Seems like a man should end up with something more for all his hard work."

"He should that," seconded Wanagan.

"Me, I worked lots of years in the camps skidding logs.

Sawdust Fires   135

You wouldn't think to look at me but I was a good skidder. Lots of men moved logs faster than me, but at the end of the day none of 'em could say I wasn't a man. And when we went into town at the end of the season nobody could say I wasn't a man there either. I drank my share and handled myself okay when the fights started. Course in no time all my money would be gone. I believe if I had the chance to do it all again I'd save some of what I earned in the camps."

Sure you would, Petronius wanted to say. You proved that with your fool night on Halsted Street. But he found the man hard to dislike as he babbled on congenially.

"That's why I took the money for setting the fire. I never did anything illegal before, but it seems like a fella should end up with a bit more for his work than just being able to say he was a man once."

"I drunk up a good share of what I earned too," rasped Wanagan. "But I still wouldn't go agin the law for money like you done."

Bennett wasn't deflated by the criticism. "You know something gentlemen? In three days time it's my birthday. On April 28th I'll be 62 years old. I don't look so old do I? How about you fellas? When are your birthdays?"

"In the winter sometime," said Wanagan. "Don't know what day. Don't care."

"What's your age?" Bennett persisted.

"Must be near 70."

"How about you Pete?"

"I'll be 27 in June."

"For gosh sakes, to be 27 again. I was full of sap at 27. Now you, Orville, you must have cut quite an impressive figure at 27."

"I could walk near 40 miles a day back then," Wanagan said with some pride.

"I believe it. I believe it. Enjoy being young Pete. When you get old and broken down like Orville and me here life is a hard pull. A hard pull."

Petronius didn't feel all that young just then. For him, being young was life before his twisted arm.

As he got Bennett onto his horse again, Petronius put a challenge to the man. "I want you to tell me one particular fact which proves it all happened just like you said."

"Ah, well, that's not so easy. I'll need some time to think of what that would be. But think on it I will."

The next leg of the journey was ridden in gathering darkness and mostly silence. Bennett and Petronius at times drifted off to sleep and had to catch themselves from slipping out of their saddles. Even the phlegmatic Wanagan seemed to nod off at times though he never lost his unerring direction.

At Wanagan's shack Bennett immediately installed himself on the bunk while the other two stayed outside to talk. In his anger Wanagan became articulate. "Now why aren't we going direct to St. Ignace?"

"I'm thinking we shouldn't take Bennett straight back."

Wanagan was outraged. "He ain't turned your head with all his friendliness has he?"

"It has to do with the trouble he'll bring down on the Driscolls."

"He might be makin' up his story to scare you off. You think of that?"

"Possible, but I believe he's telling the truth. He couldn't have known I was connected with Addy Driscoll. And it's her I'm mostly thinking about in this matter."

"I won't be happy to see her hurt neither, but if old man Driscoll done the deed like Bennett says then let it come out. We take Bennett back and collect the reward clear and simple."

"For me there's arguments on the other side. My insurance companies won't be all that pleased. Arson will be proved but they'll have to pay off on the policy to McClatchen. Then they'll try to recover the money from

Driscoll's hide and I'm not sure he's got it."

"Don't know one of those lumbermen ain't got plenty put aside."

"That's possible."

"What are you proposing we do?"

"I'd like to store Bennett here at your shack for a few days while I go back down to Muskegon and tell Addy of this. I'd like her to have some say before it's decided." Even in the dark Petronius could sense the extent of Wanagan's scowl. "I don't want her to think she wasn't consulted in a matter this important," he added.

Of course there was more to it than that. Petronius had in mind to make a bit more than the reward money on this situation. He wouldn't pressure Driscoll, that'd be blackmail. He'd just let things flow naturally. He thought of bringing Wanagan into the plan but realized the man wouldn't bend to anything shady.

Wanagan had adopted an angry silence.

Petronius tried to smooth the man's feathers. "We'll figure out some way of getting the reward money to you regardless of what happens. You got that coming for your work."

"You got a thousand dollars?"

"I haven't."

"Well then."

"If this goes bad I lose my part of the reward too, remember."

There was more silence from Wanagan. Finally he said, "I ain't agreein' to it."

With nothing settled they went into the shack and tried to sleep. Bennett seemed to be doing fine, snoring away on the bunk. But Petronius and Wanagan dozed fitfully on the rough floor, at times kicking each other in their turnings.

In the morning Petronius and Wanagan continued their argument outside the shack. "Why don't we first get him safe to the jail in Muskegon?" asked Wanagan. "You could have your talks with Addy Driscoll after that."

"Couldn't do that without letting the story out. I don't want McClatchen to get wind of this yet."

They argued on but Petronius was unshakeable in his resolve. Finally Wanagan said in defeat, "I guess I ain't got no choice. Can't get Bennett down there by myself."

"I'll leave you $20 for expenses. You want my revolver?"

"Keep your pistol. I ain't never used one. I'll trust the wrist manacles to hold Bennett."

Petronius thought of taking Wanagan's bottle of whiskey and emptying it on the ground as a further safeguard. Instead he promised to travel quickly and come back just as soon as Addy had been told. He felt a twinge of sympathy for Wanagan as he started out.

SORROW

Life is but a strife;
*   'Tis a bubble, 'tis a dream*
And man is just a little boat
*   That paddles down the stream.*
And pleasure is the waterman
*   That floats you down the tide;*
The passengers are smiling joys,
*   While sorrow sits beside.*

Muskegon Daily Chronicle

Ch 20

Petronius returned by the most direct route, arriving in Muskegon by train just after 4PM. No time for shaving or washing up. He found Addy busy at a typewriter in her father's office and motioned her outside. When they had gotten some ways down the sidewalk he came out with it.

"We found the watchman just as Wanagan claimed and the man admitted setting the fire too. But it wasn't McClatchen's doing at all. Your father paid to have it done. That's what the watchman says."

Addy slowed almost to a stop and then resumed her pace with a pained expression. "You're sure he's being truthful?"

"Fairly sure. Now, I didn't bring the man back with me. He's stashed at Wanagan's shack. Something as serious as this I wanted you to have a chance to decide. Wanagan wouldn't have much objection to letting the fellow go if you're of a mind to hush things up. Course he'll still be expecting his reward money. We'll need to talk to your father of course."

She shook her head repeatedly as they continued walking.

"Would you want some time to consider?" he asked.

"No," she shook her head several more times. "It will have to be faced. Bring the watchman back. I'll talk to my father this evening."

"I think we should talk to your father first, get his side of things."

"Perhaps you're right."

"I'll get myself a bath and clean clothes," he said.

But a telegram awaited Petronius as he reached his rooming house. It was from Wanagan and read: "Tricked me & escaped. What of reward now?"

Well, I may have mucked this up, thought Petronius as he stuffed the telegram in his pocket. Hopefully it could be salvaged.

He found Addy back at her typewriter and showed her the telegram. "Would be easy to just let things stay put now," he suggested. "Not tell anyone."

"No, it doesn't change what's happened," she answered in a sad voice. She asked that he come to the house to meet with her father."

The three of them took separate seats in the library. Mr. Driscoll pulled out a cigar, as if prepared to welcome good news.

"I'll get right to the point," said Petronius. You're aware, sir, of the reward offered for the two watchmen on duty the night of the McClatchen mill fire?"

Driscoll nodded without a great show of interest.

"One of them's been found. An old timber walker named Wanagan spotted him."

"Oh?" Driscoll perked up. "Found where?"

"Upper Peninsula. I'm just back from there. He told me something strange, this man Bennett did. That's the watchman's name, Bennett. He said he and his partner started the fire at the mill but not by McClatchen's orders. According to Bennett you gave them a sizeable sum of money to do the

Sawdust Fires   141

job. Says the fire was part of your payback to McClatchen over business disputes."

"Ha! Of course he would be sayin' something like that. He's McClatchen's man and still in the pay of McClatchen. Could you expect him to do different?

"He presented me with a story in some detail. Far as I could tell he didn't slip up. Not that I'm a flawless investigator."

"The man's had weeks to invent and polish his tale and who could be blamin' him."

"Bennett's a conniver I give you that. Always looking to give himself an escape hole if the game goes sour."

Driscoll took a second to light his cigar. "Of course he is. We can take it as just that and no more. Connivin'. In any case I'm thankful to you young man for bringin' it to my attention, though I'm doubtful any action is needed." He got to his feet to signal an end to the meeting.

"Would you mind telling me," Petronius went on, "if something is in your safe. Bennett said you have a room divider in your office which blocks the view of the safe. But when you were getting the money out he crept up and got himself a peek through. You have a fancy tobacco can, he claims, of an odd brand not made for years. I copied the name." He presented Driscoll with a slip of paper.

Driscoll sat himself down again in his chair. He crossed one leg over the other and leaned back to study the paper. One boot began to twitch. He finally looked up but said nothing, only sent a black look over to Addy as if she had organized some conspiracy. She sat quiet with her jaw out a bit.

At length Petronius said, "What remains now is deciding what you'll do about this."

"Ah," the man recovered a bit. "We could send that fellow Wanagan his share of reward money if you're sure he'll be insistin' on it. As for the night watchman, he don't want to be found anyway. We're safe with him. There's really not much that needs...."

"No, father," Addy spoke in a controlled voice. "That's not what we mean. You must report what you've done, to the police, or somebody. This has to come out."

Petronius was about to object but held his tongue.

Driscoll puffed on his cigar and blew several clouds of smoke in her direction. "Alright," he said with considerable heat. "I'll go to confession if you like. If that will clear your conscience I'd be willin' to do that."

She sighed. "I'd be happy if you went to confession. It will be good for you I'm sure, and I have no doubt the priest will insist you tell the legal authorities as part of your penance."

"Don't be too sure of that, Addy girl. You can never be sure with those priests. It depends on their mood as to what penance they'll be handin' out. I might only get a half dozen rosaries."

She straightened further in her chair. "Oh, father. Are you even taking this seriously?"

"As seriously as heart failure, Addy girl. I'm tellin' you this can't come out. I won't let it. This will ruin me as complete as a man can be ruined. It will affect you too. You should know that. You won't be livin' in this grand house or wearin' silk underthings."

"You simply cannot hide it," she argued. "And I'm aware of what will happen. Terrible things. Worse for you than for me."

Humiliated! Made a joke! Sent to jail probably!"

"We can survive. I'll help you. We can start fresh someplace. We can rebuild your business when it comes time for that."

"And what if I'm sayin' no? What then?" He looked at her hard and blew another stream of smoke.

"Then," in a small but steady voice, "I will report it."

Sawdust Fires 143

His face twisted. "You'd be helpin' McClatchen would you? That odious snake who reneged me and cheated me. You'd be on his side?"

"No!"

"Do you hate me so much for what small failures I've done ya?"

"I don't want to help McClatchen or hurt you either," she pleaded. "But it's something you've got to face. You can make restitution and be forgiven."

"Forgiven!" He got to his feet and fired the cigar into the cold fireplace.

"Poppa, poppa, poppa," cried Addy in a childlike voice.

"Addy, Addy, Addy," he mimicked as he strode angrily out of the room. They heard him leave the house with a bang of the front door.

Addy sat down on the floor. After a minute she pulled herself together. "We'll give this a day or two don't you think? What do you think?"

"Do I think he'll come forward and admit his deed?"

"I suppose that's what I mean."

"I'm not so good judge of people, but I'd say no."

"What should we do?"

"Just like you said. Wait a couple days for this to go down better with him. Then we'll see how it looks."

But they weren't to have a couple of days. The following morning some boatmen found Terence Driscoll floating in Muskegon Lake off one of the lumber piers, his body buoyed up by two nearly empty bottles in his coat pockets. Death by misadventure was the official term used by the police, covering a range of possibilities.

As soon as Petronius heard he headed to the Driscoll house, though he dreaded being the carrier of this latest bad news. He was relieved to find Addy had already gotten the report from the foreman at the mill. Petronius found her in the library with an opened scrapbook. She appeared to have cried but not heavily.

"Deepest regrets to you naturally," Petronius began awkwardly. "Your father had to get his revenge on McClatchen and didn't...." He sputtered to a stop. "Well, those aren't the things to talk about now are they?" He pointed to the scrapbook to change the subject "Do you mind if I look?"

The pages showed mementoes and photographs of the Driscoll family in happier times. One particular picture caught his eye, of father and daughter posing formally in front of a snow fort, with Addy about 10 years old, already tall and with a self satisfied smile. The picture was probably from the lumber camp.

"He froze me in his mind somehow just like in that photograph," she said. "A little girl forever and not to be taken seriously in the adult world. I would have helped him if he'd let me. I pushed him too hard on this, I know."

"You did the right thing I'd say. I'm not sure I have. Should have brought Bennett straight back like Wanagan wanted. Let the police and court take it. Might have come out different."

"You wanted to spare me as much as possible and I'm grateful."

He handed the scrapbook back with a feeling of chagrin. "Got a painful confession to make on that. Truth is I wanted to put you in a hard fix. Make you decide one way or the other. Would have gloated a little if you'd chose to cover it up and save yourself and your father."

"Oh," she said softly. Her face sagged a little. "It hurts to have you tell me that."

"Hurts to admit it."

He could feel she sensed the extent of his duplicity, though perhaps not the worst of it. He mumbled an apology and quietly left the house, sure she would want no further dealings with him.

Sawdust Fires   145

But the following day she sent a note asking for his assistance. When they met at in the Driscoll Company office, Addy was already dressed in mourning black. She explained. "Could you notify the authorities as to my father's part in the arson? The police and court will have to be told I suppose. You'll know better than I how to go about it. That would take a considerable weight off me while I make funeral arrangements and try to keep the business going."

"You wouldn't rather wait for that whole affair to come out until after the funeral?"

"I'd rather face it all now. I don't want false eulogies for my father. And there are rumors floating about anyway."

"I'll be more than pleased to handle that side of things for you."

She extended her hand in a businesslike manner. "I'd be grateful."

Petronius immediately visited the local police station. To his frustration he faced continued hostility. The officer he talked to said they welcomed any information he could offer but would need to conduct their own investigation to find the real facts of the case.

Next Petronius made a statement at the newspaper office, hoping to get the least sensational report into print. But the newspaper quickly dispatched a reporter to question Addy and any others willing to talk. The story the next day appeared under the heading "Tale of Intrigue," and included more speculation than fact.

On the same day Petronius wired his insurance companies in Chicago with a summary of events. Almost immediately he received a telegram back, about which he approached Addy. He found her at her father's old desk in the lumber company office, sorting through correspondence and trying to tuck back some strands of loose hair.

"Got a wire from the insurance companies asking for some estimate of your father's worth," he said. "They're looking to attach assets to cover what they'll pay out on the McClatchen fire. What should I tell them?"

"I've had no chance to do any real examination of the books. If you can stall them until after the funeral I'd be grateful."

He agreed.

Lastly Petronius sent a letter to McClatchen. "Since all has come out in your favor," he began, "would you be willing to turn over the cash reward to Orville Wanagan? He's the man you can thank for collecting your insurance monies."

He got back a note from McClatchen's secretary regretting that the terms of the reward hadn't strictly been met, and so no monies could be tendered. Petronius crumpled the note and kicked it towards a dustbin, symbolic of his last few days efforts.

An elderly aunt on Addy's mother's side had come from Massachusetts for the wake and funeral. Tall and gangly, like Addy, she appeared ready to assume the role of pillar of strength, but Addy didn't need much propping up. Harried from all sides she went about her tasks with seeming calm and directness. And on the day of the funeral she presented an elegant picture in her long black dress. The veil she wore worked to her advantage, hiding her face enough so anyone unfamiliar with her looks would have assumed a lovely visage.

Besides her aunt, Addy was joined in the front pew of the church by Sam Washoo, Joshua's mother, Mrs. Fogarty and the mill foreman. Petronius felt comfortable in the back. He was rather surprised at how comfortable he did feel in the church. He suspected it was the parish priest, a gruff but approachable fellow named Van Grough, and like Brubacher, a Dutchman. He had talked some with the man during the wake. Although the manner of Driscoll's death appeared damning, Van Grough had insisted on extending every benefit of the Church. Perhaps it was in deference to Addy. In any case, Driscoll would be sent to his rest with a Mass of Benediction and afterwards buried in St. Mary's cemetery.

Van Grough began his sermon in a slow and accented voice. "Who knows why people do the things dey do?" He went on to ask for God's mercy on Terence Brendan Driscoll's soul, "knowing we ourselves vil one day have to call on dat same mercy."

The priest noted some happier times in Driscoll's life. Apparently the Irishman had been fair, and at times generous, to his employees. In earlier years he had served on several public improvement committees. St. Patrick's day had been his special joy and he had been a great promoter of that day's festivities. And of course he had raised a loving daughter.

Petronius looked about. There were maybe seven dozen people at the funeral, about half of them Driscoll employees, he judged. He noted five or six mill owners had come, though none of the biggest. No Crisp or Talman or Detwiler. McClatchen had sent a spray of flowers earlier to the house with a ribbon which read, "Fellow Lumberman." Whether the message represented an expression of compassion or a crow of triumph Petronius couldn't guess.

A couple of Indian families, evidently acquaintances of Addy, attended also, but insisted on staying at the back of the church. Petronius had looked for Joshua at some point but had seen nothing of the boy during the several days' proceedings.

The rather chilly sun had about reached its noon peak as the funeral procession wound into St. Mary's cemetery, made green and inviting by recent rains. As the final words were spoken and the casket let down into the ground, Addy gave a tiny lurch but caught herself and preserved the demeanor she had maintained throughout.

There was already an aged stone at the plot. The grey obelisk had been there since the death of Addy's mother nearly 20 years earlier, long enough to have been smoothed by the rain and settle itself into the sod with a slight tilt. And so Driscoll joined the Mahoneys, the Murphys and the Moriaritys, the O'Briens, the O'Boyles and the O'Neils, a less exclusive membership than the Muskegon Club.

In the next week, as he walked about the lake or played cards, Petronius did a lot of thinking about Terence Driscoll's failed revenge, and his own hoped for day of reckoning in Chicago. He began to have a change of heart, although his thoughts didn't come out all that profound or coherent.

Life dealt plenty of hard blows, that much he knew. And it was easy to be hard in return, to deal blow for blow. Natural even. Still, it appeared to be a choice. And if the heaven he and Addy had felt was real, if there was a place God meted out justice, then there was no need to settle old scores here in this world.

His new slant gave him some comfort. But the gap between himself and Addy bothered him. And there seemed no way of healing it. Earlier he had been sure when the time came to distance himself from Addy Driscoll he could do it without a second thought. Now he felt differently.

THE WATER PROBLEM

It seems as though the time had come for providing a proper water supply, not by voting a large sum in the dark, but by having the merits of one or more feasible plans properly considered.

Muskegon Daily Chronicle

Ch 21

It was barely past ten when Petronius was awakened by the clanging of fire bells. He had intended to sleep late on this Saturday morning, but now his immediate thought was of another sawmill ablaze. He leaped for his clothes. As he struggled into his shirt he could hear the clamor growing and it seemed to come from many parts of town. Soon not just alarm bells but whistles from the sawmills began to shriek. He was just at the door of the rooming house when church bells also joined in. Whatever was happening was more than a small fire.

As he went into the street he noted the unusual warmth of the air for the middle of May. A strong wind was blowing, out of the north he judged. He really had no need to ask the direction of the fire; only to follow the stream of people, some running like children, others in a slow walk, as if they feared what they might find. They went down Western Avenue to Pine Street, then a block south. Petronius could see billows of smoke and flame with the attending commotion of people and fire apparatus.

The blaze had taken strong hold. Several buildings, mostly businesses, had already been consumed and a half dozen others burned furiously. Gusts from the strong winds regularly launched flights of sparks and flaming debris into the air.

The crowd felt they should be doing something to help

but all they could do was watch and talk, so they milled about and argued loudly. Petronius heard disagreements as to the source of the fire. Some claimed it had started at a blacksmith shop. Others said the blacksmith hadn't been at his shop, nor any fire left in his forge. No, it had been careless smokers at Emory's Livery Barn. Yet another faction said a drunk, angered at his rough treatment the night before, had set fire to McCuddy's saloon. In any case the call for help had already gone out to Grand Rapids.

Petronius took out paper and noted some things down. He'd have to make a report to the insurance companies. He pushed his way closer to the action. In front of him a tall man in a suit stomped about, looking at once official and combative. "Now we'll pay," he exclaimed. "The whole town will pay. How many times did I argue for a new waterworks? Always turned down!" He positively invited anyone to debate the issue. But none did. The puny streams of water coming from some of the fire hoses made the case. If things got worse water would have to be pumped directly from the lake, all agreed. But that presented difficulties also. A powerful pumper would have to be brought in from somewhere, and lots of hose would have to be diverted to cover the great distance from the lake front.

An even more serious discussion raged amongst Chief Bonner and his fire fighters. Where could they best concentrate their efforts? Should they construct a strong fire line to the south, thus protecting the courthouse and large residences in that direction? But how could they just ignore these raging flames here? If not dampened, the fire brands hurled into the air would surely start additional fires.

Advice came from every side, including screams from those whose establishments were nearby. Finally the fire chief divided his force in half; one group to fight the flames at hand, the other to build a barricade of thoroughly wetted buildings to the south, against which the fire, if not checked at its

Sawdust Fires   151

source, would likely burn out.

The wind failed to cooperate. At times it blew in furious gusts which made the flames snap and roar like stoked coals in a metal forge. Just then a large frame building, a rooming house Petronius guessed, collapsed into itself, sending a cloud of sparks and hot tinders in all directions. The people leaped away, with some individuals slapping frantically as embers lighted on their clothing. Petronius decided to move to the south, to gauge the success of the other group of fire fighters.

As soon as he got downwind of the flames he could feel the immense heat being generated. The smoke however was not thick nor overpowering. With the powerful wind the fire burned efficiently. In fact he found the smell of the smoke almost pleasant, remindful of the fires in kitchen stoves.

Petronius had been at his new observation post only a few minutes when a shout went up. A flaming piece of tar paper had sailed completely over the wetted structures and set some shingles ablaze on a roof further south. The news of this seemed to telegraph back instantly and the crowd reacted with howls of dismay. One of the stronger hoses was immediately turned on this new little blaze with good effect. But the breech of defenses threw confusion and questioning into the men's efforts. Had they set up their line too close? Were they just wasting water on buildings which dried too quickly in the hot gale sweeping over everything? Someone pointed to a roof where moisture evaporated visibly with clouds of steam. The question was -- did they have the resources to contain this fire? Petronius felt he knew the answer and he set out at a dash for Addy's house.

The residences he passed varied in their states of alarm. Some occupants stood on upper balconies looking unconcerned, as if watching a fireworks demonstration. Others prepared for departure. Wagons waited at the curb with horses hitched, or were pulled close to front steps. A few had been run up alongside windows so furniture could be handed out.

When he reached the mansions of Addy's block he noted several attempts to nail wetted blankets onto the high roofs. Servants and handymen worked from extension ladders or crawled precariously onto the roof surfaces. While he watched, a blanket was whipped out of a man's hand and took sail. It was not just the wind but the angles and complexities of those roofs which made the effort look hopeless.

He found Addy at the side of the house with Mrs. Fogarty, dipping quilts into a tub of water.

"I'm so glad you came. I expect Sam but he hasn't arrived yet." She gave him time to catch his breath before asking, "Is the fire as bad as everyone says?"

"Very bad and headed this way."

She looked up towards the top of the house. "Should we try to get these quilts onto the roof somehow? The neighbors all say... "

He shook his head. "No use to that. Wet quilts won't help. Water hoses won't help. This fire is going to take everything and your house is in the path of it."

She looked utterly unbelieving for a second. "Then what should we do?"

"Decide what to save right now and I'll help you load it into your wagon."

Mrs. Fogarty faced him with a scowl. "Are ya sayin' young man we should be leavin' this house without so much as a fight?"

"I'm saying, Mrs. Fogarty, the men fighting this fire can't stop it. Nothing will until it runs out of buildings to burn."

With that he went to the stable. Again his bad arm hampered action, but the horse cooperated and he eventually hitched the animal properly between the stays and backed the vehicle out into the yard.

A few items had been brought out and set in a pile

Sawdust Fires 153

including a family album, a stack of books and a small wooden chest, probably silverware. Addy's cat, Muriel, peered out of a bushel basket padded with burlap.

Petronius went into the house to move things along. Mrs. Fogarty was all abustle but Addy was nowhere to be seen.

"With my arm I can't do much hauling," yelled Petronius up the stairs. "Maybe you could send for some of your mill workers." He called out again but got no answer from Addy. He finally found her on the third floor looking out onto a small screened porch. "My girl friends and I often slept here on summer evenings. We pretended to be in a high tree house."

Addy would not be hurried as she moved slowly from room to room. She seemed not so much in a dilemma at what to take as wishing to visit the memories of each room.

They were in the dining room boxing up some china when Sam walked in. Addy immediately became more businesslike. After she had thanked him for coming she said, "I'll tell you the same as Mrs. Fogarty. Take whatever you wish from the house for yourself or your family. Now, has Joshua come with you?"

"Joshua went out very early my daughter says. He may be watching the fire or somewheres in the woods hunting. We don't know." He waved his hand towards the table and chairs. "What would you have me move first?"

She convinced him she was not interested in saving the larger pieces of furniture. Rather he should first go down to the basement and pick out some tools for himself.

A man ran down the street announcing in a loud voice the court house was going up.

"Oh, my." Addy looked almost joyful. "Let's go watch for a few minutes." She pulled Petronius's good arm.

They ran like children the two blocks to court house square. The two story structure burned like a beacon, the flames on the peaked roof lighting the elegant cupola with its tall windows. Many of the large surrounding trees also blazed, their fresh green leaves and blossoms no retardant to the consuming heat.

Serious resistance by the fire fighters had collapsed. The best they could do was preserve hoses and equipment. They also warned residents and helped with evacuations where they could. The fire would run its course now.

Addy and Petronius went back towards her house at a brisk walk rather than a run. They observed panic in the actions of the people. Ahead a wagon, dangerously overloaded, teetered and then toppled, causing nearby horses to rear in confusion amongst the rolling barrels and furnishings.

Everywhere they saw oddities. Someone tossed a large fancy mirror out of an upstairs window to smash senselessly on the ground. A woman brought out a pan of dishwater and set it in the middle of the sidewalk. When a man running past upset the pan the woman gave furious chase, flinging a dish rag

Back at the house Sam had rigged some uprights on the wagon so it could be loaded higher. He had also located a tarp and some rope.

The Stimson house was the first in the block to burst into flame. Everyone paused from their loading and went outside to look.

"Is that little Melissa standing near the house?" Addy questioned. "What is she doing and where are her parents?" Before answers could be voiced, an older girl bolted out of the house, the hem of her dress ablaze. Petronius grabbed up one of the still damp quilts and started over.

"Penelope here!" Addy called. "This way!"

But the shrieking child flew towards the street. Petronius leaped a fish pond and charged through a grove of lilacs in pursuit, overtaking the girl just as the flames caught in her hair. Bowling her over with the quilt, he quickly snuffed out the fire but the child's gasping cries continued.

Sawdust Fires 155

Addy was quickly beside him. "How badly is she burned?" They carefully peeled away the quilt and some pieces of charred dress revealing several raw patches. "Yes," she concluded. "She needs a doctor."

Little Melissa now joined them, screaming and crying almost as much as her sister. When Addy had restored calm she got the story. The Stimson family had left the house much earlier but Melissa had forgotten her doll. The two girls, unknown to their parents, had slipped back to retrieve it. Now Penelope clutched the doll to herself as if it were her own treasure.

Removing the potted plants from a small wagon they bundled Penelope in the quilt and placed her into the conveyance. In spite of all the heat the girl shivered in pain.

"I ask you and Sam to do what you can for my things here, said Addy. "Mrs Fogarty and I will take Penelope for help." Without further discussion they went off with Addy pulling and Mrs Fogarty alongside the wagon, holding the burned child's hand to comfort. Melissa trailed, not sure whether to skip happily with her regained doll in hand or résumé crying.

Petronius helped Sam get the loaded wagon under way and into the fleeing stream of traffic. Sam would head east of town and store the goods at his farm . The cat could be heard meowing as cinders pattered down on the tarp.

It was not too long before each gust of wind brought showers of embers and flaming pieces and Petronius knew he had only minutes now. He had the feeling they had not done a proper job. In the house he dashed up to Addy's bedroom. What did she really need here which could still be saved? Using a blanket as a hamper he tossed in a pair of dresses, some underclothes and a hair brush. Down in the south sitting room he saw Addy's easel and the folders holding her sketches. He grabbed the pictures and added them to his baggage.

He paused outside. All of the mansions had fires of some sort dancing on their roofs now. Trees burned as well, and even the gazebo in the center of the park. He set the blanket down and watched for a minute before the heat became overpowering. Some of the flames looked almost beautiful among the tall chimneys and turrets. He wondered if Addy wished she could sketch this momentous time. As he looked towards the business section and the main body of the fire he noticed some of the paving in the street and sidewalks. The hexagonal slabs of cedar were burning. Not the edges, which were still damp with dirt and moss, but the centers, making the wood chunks look like giant votive candles.

As Petronius walked south, out of range of the flames, carrying his clumsy cargo, he wondered what time it was. The smoke-filled sky gave no indication. He realized he hadn't shaved or eaten anything. But he felt relieved to know he would have a bed to sleep in that night. Many would not.

IN RUINS

The devouring element, the fire fiend, has swept down upon us with a fury unprecedented.

Muskegon Daily Chronicle

Ch 22

As the day wore on the wind began to let up. Petronius returned to his rooming house, stored Addy's blanket full of things near his bunk and went downstairs for food. Mrs. Charlton had eliminated fixed meals but set out plates of sandwiches and pitchers of tea. Petronius was glad to sprawl in a chair for a short rest. He then headed for the hospital.

Doctors and nurses moved about busily in the small building, but seemed to have things well in hand. Apparently not many injuries had been caused by the fire. Petronius inquired after Addy and the Stimson child. Both had left. The burned girl had been salved, bandaged and returned to the care of her family.

After an hour's search Petronius found Addy passing out coffee and tea at a relief tent set up by the Salvation Army. He told her about the blanket full of her clothes and other articles.

"Oh thank you. I'm not thinking clearly and it never occurred to me to take things to wear tomorrow."

"Did you go back to have a look at the fire?" Petronius asked.

Addy shook her head.

"I wish I could tell you the wind shifted and your house was spared. But all your block got swept away."

She acknowledged the news with a weak smile.

"It seems being a detective hired to investigate fires I'd be of more use during a fire."

"But what can you do? There's no stopping the fire, just as you said."

"I would have saved your house if I'd known how."

She reached out and grabbed his hand. "Oh, I know you would and I'm grateful. You did a lot. The Stimson family sends thanks. You're the one who saved Penelope."

"She'll recover okay will she?"

"There'll be some painful weeks and lasting scars, but yes."

He held her hand for a few seconds without speaking.

"I've heard they're asking for men down by the lake to help connect hoses," she said.

"Well then, I'll go down there."

A steam dredge had been brought in close to shore and rigged with a large pump. More coils of hose were coming in from surrounding towns and the fire chief hoped to run a double line of hoses the entire way from the lake to the fire. It seemed a far shot but at least the fire fighters had a plan to follow and they went about it with energy. Petronius did what he could to help drag the heavy sections of hose up the streets but his one-handed efforts were looked upon as no better than the help of a child. He couldn't assist at all with the couplings.

It took them more than an hour to cover the mile distance but when the water began to surge through the throbbing hoses it gave the fire fighters a renewed sense of mission. Now they had a serious weapon against the fire.

But before they could get into proper position the wind shifted about and began to blow again with renewed fury, sending the fire back almost in the same the direction it had come, and right into the faces of the fire fighters.

The increased water supply wasn't enough. By directing both hoses at the same point they could hold back the fire in the middle but could do nothing to stem advance around the flanks. Word went back to turn off the pump and the men began hurriedly uncoupling hose in preparation for another retreat. Petronius helped by stomping the water out of the hose sections so they could be rolled up and transported out of danger.

Mill hands and boomers took turns fighting the fire. All the men and hoses did slow the progress of the fire, but the ferocious wind drove the flames on. By nightfall the blaze had burned a parallel swath almost back to its start and was striking into new territory to the north.

Many who still had homes refused to go to them for fear the fire would turn in their direction and catch them sleeping. The only safe thing was to keep an eye on it. Petronius found himself among the watchers, although his fascination with the flames had long since spent itself. His clothes had become layered with motes of soot and his eyes began seeing bright spots of orange even when closed. Addy watched with him for a time but then went back to St. Mary's church to sleep. A number of churches and public buildings, those constructed of brick, had been thrown open to receive the homeless for the night.

At last the fire burned itself out against the lake, but not before wiping out a half dozen sawmills and their great stacks of lumber. Petronius felt some relief Addy had not witnessed her father's mill being consumed. Someone announced the time as a quarter short of 2AM. Petronius looked back along the path of the fire and saw tiny glowing embers still nourished by the wind. Yet everyone felt the fire was at last over and they trudged off to whatever beds they could find. Petronius went to his rooming house, which still survived.

The next morning Petronius arrived at St. Mary's early with Addy's change of clothing. He saw an unusual scene for a church. The confessionals had become changing rooms and people continued to sleep stretched out on the pews as the eight o'clock Mass started. He joined Addy in one of the pews towards the front.

No mention of the fire was made during the Mass until the sermon. Then Father Van Grough offered his condolences to all who had suffered loss, and assured those present, that even in the midst of calamity, the Lord remained their friend. But many would need human friends in the weeks ahead, he went on, and urged any who had the resources to be one of those helping friends. A special collection would be taken up the following Sunday.

After the Mass Addy and Petronius joined the crowds looking over the carnage. Sightseers had come by train from as far away as Lansing. The top attraction seemed to be the large house burned strangely in half from top to bottom, marking the point the wind and flames had reached before suddenly shifting into reverse. Also popular was the ice house. It's roof and walls had burned totally away, leaving exposed a huge glistening pile of crystal blocks, the edges all rounded and dripping from the heat. Yet another point of interest, at least for the locals, was the McClatchen property. Despite it's spacious grounds McClatchen's grand mansion and stables had been leveled. But he had marshaled enough manpower and wagons to save the furnishings and valuables.

Overall there was little dramatic to see. Mostly the eye found block after block of ashes and smoldering piles of boards with only chimneys and blackened tree trucks left upright. Some families sifted through the remains of their houses looking for something to salvage.

A few fire fighters trained streams of water on the remaining hot spots, mostly places where thick layers of sawdust had been deposited over the years. The men looked chagrined as well as tired. Though certainly not blamed for the lack of containment, no one considered them heroes either. They had tried but the fire had bested their every move.

A special two page edition of The Muskegon Chronicle was being hawked by newsboys. The newspaper estimated nearly 400 buildings had been consumed in what it called "The Great Gale of a Fire." A rough map described the area of devastation, including numerous residences, a sizeable chunk of the business section and nearly a dozen sawmills and manufacturing plants.

Predictably an editorial raged against the lack of foresight in providing an adequate waterworks. Another article urged residents and business people to rebuild quickly on a larger and grander scale, using stone and brick to guarantee the permanence of future structures.

But rumors dampened enthusiasm for rebuilding. Many of the destroyed buildings had been insured but now talk went around the losses were heavy enough to force the fire insurance companies into bankruptcy. Another of the rumors suggested the lumbermen would use the fire as an excuse to close their mills and head west, especially those who had lost residences, like McClatchen. If the lumbermen pulled out who would have money to rebuild?

McCuddy's Saloon, at least, had acted on the "rebuild" theme, erecting a tent and rough tables on its former site. Signs advertised a "fire sale" on beer drawn from barrels which had, so McCuddy claimed, miraculously survived in the building's basement. For this day the Sunday closing law was ignored. A festive air was being attempted but not with complete success. Those tipping glasses of beer seemed more somber than merry.

A couple of other large tents were being set up and would provide meals later in the day for the homeless. All expense was being picked up by Mrs. McClatchen a worker said. Petronius felt surprise. Mrs. McClatchen? He couldn't imagine the existence of a Mrs. McClatchen.

"What's she like?" he asked Addy, "The wife of McClatchen?"

"I know her only a little. She stays very much in the background even when sponsoring social events."

They walked down near the lake front to inspect the remains of the sawmills. It was impossible for Petronius to tell which site had contained the Driscoll mill but Addy went

Sawdust Fires 162

right to the spot. She examined the scene from several sides. A few pieces of machinery poked up from the debris, the twisted metal already browned with rust. It was obvious nothing could be salvaged. He watched her face carefully. Her jaw thrust out a bit but her eyes showed little emotion.

"What do you plan to do now?" he asked as they walked away from the site.

"I'd like to help some of the homeless if I can. I liked Father Van Grough's sermon on being a friend to those most in need."

Petronius started to protest. She was still talking like a wealthy person. What did she have left? A few logs floating in the mill pond and some timber up north. Wouldn't add up to one quarter of her father's debts. But this seemed hardly the day to face all the realities.

"Here's an idea," he said. "Some time back you said you'd show me your personal pine stand in Newaygo County. Might be just the day to do that. I'll see to renting a carriage if you agree."

She visibly brightened. "Walking among those trees always lifts me up. Yes, I'd like to do that."

Petronius secured a pair of Mrs. Charlton's sandwiches and filled a bottle of water. He had to wait a bit at the livery stable before one of the out of town sightseers turned in a carriage.

In the country the signs of Spring again prevailed. Though their clothes still smelled of ashes the country air delighted their nostrils. They could see an occasional flash of Dogwood and catch the fragrance of honeysuckle. Green showed everywhere. Both quickly grew sleepy and they alternated handling the reins while the other dozed.

The 40 acres of pine was well away from the river, so not very accessible. They had to tether the horse and walk the last half mile.

When they came over a ridge in sight of the property

Sawdust Fires   163

Addy's face took on a stricken look and her voice held alarm. "Somebody's been pirating timber."

When they got closer they could see stumps of trees and ruts where logs had been dragged out. She stopped to examine the track left by a large cleated wheel. "They used a steam tractor," she muttered.

The tracks looked a week or two old to Petronius. Evidently when word had gotten out lumberman Driscoll was dead the timber was considered fair game. A young daughter would be no obstacle.

"We might better stop here," Petronius cautioned, catching her arm. But Addy insisted on going to the spot of her favorite tree . A stalk of splintered wood reached several feet above the rest of the large stump, indicating the tree hadn't come down clean. Cuttings from the top and limbs lay scattered about, still green with needles. Addy began to cry and her demolished face became that of an inconsolable child. Sobs shook her shoulders and buckled her knees until she huddled on the ground. Petronius knelt beside her and put his arm tightly about her as if it was the only way she could survive the ordeal.

When she finally accepted his offered handkerchief she said, "It's so silly to cry over something like a tree."

"That may be right," he said, "but you've had a good deal happening lately." He felt bad about bringing her here for this and tried to think of something to make amends. "I could follow the tracks of that steam tractor. Probably locate the sawmill where the logs were taken. A big tree like yours would be noted." He knew it sounded lame as he said it.

She shook her head and began to cry again quietly. "I dreamed I would build a little house someday at the very top, and watch the clouds."

"You'd have privacy at least. I wouldn't climb up there."

She had to smile a little through the tears.

As they drove back to town they talked again of what she

might do in the future.

"In the fall I believe I'd be able to get work teaching school."

"I'd say you're a natural teacher. Good with children. You'd do fine as a teacher."

"I've always thought of myself as too important to be just a school teacher. It's part of my vanity really. Because of my father's wealth I always thought myself better than others."

"In my mind you are better. You have intelligence and spirit, and a kind heart."

She didn't answer.

"Of course, we two are damaged goods, you and I." he said. "Me more than you. That's not to say I don't find you attractive. And I could use a good teacher myself. I don't have much to offer in return, except a certain loyalty. Love I should say. I'm not putting this very gracefully."

She turned to face him. "You're doing fine and it's most kind of you. I realize you may be saying all this out of sympathy for me."

"Don't believe I am, though I didn't have this in mind when we started out. We both need a day or two to think on things."

Along the way they stopped and picked some sprigs of dogwood blossoms. They again dozed and took turns holding the horse's reins. When they reached Muskegon the setting sun was putting an orange glow to the dust and smoke still in the air. Addy would again be able to spend the night in the church, but on the morrow other arrangements would have to be made.

SNUB

The Chicago Tribune, in its account of the fire, wrongly credits Muskegon with but 15,000 inhabitants and 11 churches, an account calculated to do much harm by belittling [our] city.

Muskegon Daily Chronicle

Ch 23

The following morning Petronius poked around the place where the fire was supposed to have begun. He discovered nothing in the charred boards and piles of ashes which gave any real clue to the fire's origin. Perhaps a more experienced man would have done better. On the other hand Chief Bonner, with all his expertise, seemed to have no strong opinion either, at least none he would offer to the newspapers. Petronius thought about his problem for a while. What report should he send to the insurance companies? He really couldn't tell them any more than they knew already from newspaper accounts. He finally wired only the question, "How do you wish me to proceed?"

An answer came back almost immediately, "Financial chaos here stop your services no longer needed."

Petronius sent a further inquiry as to salary still coming to him but received no reply. He stomped around the streets in anger for a time and then decided to take the street railway out to the great sand dune near Lake Michigan. The exertion of climbing the slippery pile calmed him. He found it warm at the top as long as he stayed out of the wind directly from the big lake.

Large blackened areas showed in the distance where the fire had carved through town.

He wondered what to do about Addy? He really did feel great affection for her. She could be bossy but she had a heart that was kindness through and through. His earlier feelings of antagonism towards her had been mostly due to his own shortcomings. He had been in competition with her. He had found it hard to admit she was smarter and better than him in many ways, perhaps even a better athlete now he had only one arm. He recalled when they had engaged in their little baseball game on the 4th of July. At first he had played rather condescendingly, but later had competed with all his might when her abilities began to outshine his own.

He thought he should withdraw the romantic interest he had tendered to Addy the day before. What, after all, did he have to offer now? He had no job and no prospects. The blacklist in Chicago probably still featured his name and Muskegon was a boom town headed for bust. Perhaps he should head west to Arizona where his friend Jacob Larson now lived amongst the cowboys. Petronius didn't think he had even the train fare to get to Arizona, but maybe he could borrow it from Larson. With that in mind he leaned back and took a snooze.

When Petronius awoke he had a fresh thought. Before he left, he should at least find out what had truly gone on between Terence Driscoll and Angus McClatchen. He was supposed to be a detective after all. Of course the only way to learn the answers went right through McClatchen and that could be a problem.

He considered possible moves. He thought about sending a note and wording it in such a manner as to suggest he had damaging information to present. But that immediately called to mind the note from Pattone and Shelvay of a year earlier and all its ridiculous subterfuge. He decided to be simple and direct. His note would just request a meeting, and at Mr. McClatchen's convenience.

Petronius went to McClatchen's business office on Western Avenue. It was the first time he had entered that establishment and the place gave him the impression of a lumbering museum. He saw the ends of logs scattered about, branded with their identifying marks. On the pine paneled walls hung lumbering tools and pictures showing camp scenes.

After a 15 minute wait Petronius was granted a moment with McClatchen's secretary. He handed the man his note and asked its deliverance. In turn he was informed Mr. McClatchen was vitally busy just then, preparing for his move west, and if the letter contained any request whatsoever upon Mr. McClatchen's time, well then its chances of being favored were remote, remote at best.

But to his surprise Petronius got an envelope back within an hour. It contained a note scribbled in ink saying Angus McClatchen would be happy to meet with him, and that very afternoon if the time fit Petronius' schedule.

Petronius decided it did fit.

REBUILD

Other cities all had great fires. They recovered and those cities were better than before. American pluck did this and Muskegon has as much of it to the square inch as any city to be found...................Wealthy citizens can do great good now by contributing to a fund to help the poorer families rebuild from the fire.

Muskegon Daily Chronicle

Ch 24

Petronius was admitted to McClatchen's suite at the Occidental Hotel. The man presided at a table piled high with records and account books. He rose in greeting and offered Petronius a chair.

"So ye be the talented detective from Chicago?" he said.

Petronius could detect no sarcasm in McClatchen's voice. The man just seemed to be in an affable mood. He looked his most grandfatherly in open necked shirt and rolled up sleeves.

Petronius took his seat and began. "I wish to confer with you on two points, sir, and these may take some little time."

McClatchen waved his hand for Petronius to continue.

"First then. Would you tell me the facts of the disagreement you had with Driscoll?"

McClatchen leaned back in his chair and studied Petronius for a few seconds before answering. "It started when he come over to look at the final figures on our timber deal. I could see he'd been celebrating with the bottle. Thought he'd dance an Irish jig right in my hallway. I meant to have some fun with him, let a little of the steam out of his boiler, ye might say, but it went further. "

McClatchen related the incident and Petronius filled in the particulars with his mind's eye.

Sawdust Fires 169

The two were in McClatchen's house, seated in his upstairs office, a medium sized room with its own fireplace. Light came from a single oil lamp and the glow of the fire. McClatchen sat beside his desk with one leg draped over a corner.

"This membership in the Muskegon Club, Driscoll, it may not come through."

Driscoll put down his cigar. "I don't believe I'm understandin' you."

"I'll do what I agreed to. I'll nominate you for membership and I'll vote for you. What the others will do I don't know."

"Are you saying my membership will be turned down?"

"Indeed it might."

"It was a bargain you made me, McClatchen. This membership means a lot to me."

"I made no promise you'd get in, only I'd nominate you and give you my own vote."

"You could easily influence the votes of the others, you know that."

"I could, but I'd like it to be a fair proceeding."

"Ha! Fair! So it's nominating me and voting for me but makin' clear to the others it's all a sham and you're against me! That's a fair proceedin'?"

"This lumber deal didn't make us kith and kin, Driscoll."

"I wasn't looking to be kin, only to be treated fair, like an equal."

McClatchen waved his hand dismissively. "Ah, you ain't half an equal to me. You're a bookkeeper, a clerk turned lumberman. Me, I knocked down 30 trees a day in hard winters, got to be gang boss, got to be foreman, got to be the drivingest man in 10 camps."

"I've done the things other lumberman have done, McClatchen, and I've done them well enough."

McClatchen spoke calmly, though with obvious relish.

"You done 'em when it was easy, when you already owned your own camp. And you bought the camp with your wife's money."

Driscoll's face had gone from the glow of a few drinks to a red fury and he controlled his voice with effort. "Future lumbermen will be more like me than you, McClatchen. Men who read books, understand finance and economics, not louts who know only hammerin' people down with their fists."

"I done okay with my fists and I know some finance too."

"Then get your bloody behind out to Oregon or California. They'll be choppin' you down to size."

"I mean to go to go out there and I'll do fine. You see, it ain't just finance. I understand the insides of men. Take you. You're a small man inside who wants to look big, and wants it way too much."

Driscoll fired his cigar towards the fireplace but it bounced short and scattered sparks on the carpet before smouldering out. "I won't be accepting this, McClatchen. You won't be renegin' on me."

"Ah, donna get in a fight with me, Driscoll. You know better than that."

"I mean to fight. I'll have you in court."

"Court? What court cares about membership in the Muskegon Club?"

"This will be criminal court, and them chargin' you with murder."

"What are you on about?"

"The Willard Branson business."

"You don't know nothing about that."

"Maybe I do. We'll see if I do."

McClatchen's voice changed tone. "Ya silly Irish sot. You think you can bully me? It can't be done. Not by you or anyone."

Driscoll thrust his face forward. "We'll see!"

McClatchen returned to his calm voice. "Then ye got

yourself a fight, laddie. And I say right now ye'll wait a good time for the money on this timber deal. Ye will indeed."

"Then I'll have you in court over that too."

McClatchen got up with surprising quickness and kicked Driscoll's chair over sideways. Driscoll scrambled to his feet and avoided another kick aimed at his backside. His face looked a bit stunned when he fled down the stairs, as if he hadn't expected negotiations to end so suddenly.

Petronius sat and considered the story for a time, and then asked: "This Willard Branson, who was he?"

"One of the instigators of the labor strike eight or nine years back. Worked at the log sorting grounds at the time. 'Course he weren't welcome in town after that. Then a year or so after the labor trouble I visited my number three camp, and here was this Branson a gang boss, in my own camp. He wasn't using the name Branson but I recognized him and ordered him out. He said he wouldn't go unless I put him out myself. Claimed I wasn't man enough no longer. Now it was a mistake to fight a man 30 years younger but he had a goading way about him."

"Beat you did he?"

"He weren't a large man but quick with his fists. Years earlier I would have whipped him, but time slows a man, even such as me. I bloodied him some and then he got me down and kicked in a couple of my ribs. Would have done more if the foreman hadn't pulled him off."

"How did it all end?"

"That was the end of it. Branson got his gear, left camp and I saw nothin' more of him."

"Did he brag about beating you?"

"I expect he did. I would have bragged."

"What became of Branson after that?"

"From what I heard he died in an accident at some camp in Wisconsin. Whether he stayed in labor organizing I don't know."

"Entirely an accident you say?"

McClatchen's voice stayed even and affable. "Logging is dangerous work, and accidents common enough in the woods."

Petronius pressed harder. "You'd be willing to swear on your mother's Bible it was merely an accident and you had no part in it?"

"Laddie," he said in a scolding tone, "don't be setting yourself up as some judge in a courtroom. I heard it was an accident and that's all we're likely to know of it."

Petronius moved on. "What happened further between you and Driscoll?"

"Lot's happened. He went to court over the money like he promised. Didn't get nowheres though. He hadn't gone to the trouble to get everything pinned down in writing and looked over by lawyers. So I stalled and dodged his every move. Months come and went and he needed money desperate for something. I think a payment come due for timber rights. Anyways he sent a note saying he'd take just $30,000 immediate cash to settle our deal."

"What has the total amount originally due him?"

"Little over $185,000."

"He was willing to accept only $30,000?"

"So he said. I had my lawyer prepare a paper and make him sign it before I give him the money. Course that wasn't the end of it. A short time later he calls me on my telephone saying it don't matter whether he'd signed the legal paper or not. The balance of the money was still owed to him and he meant to have it. Said he'd go to any means. I told him to take me to court but he dinna see the joke in it."

"So what did he do?"

"Nothing for some time and then he calls me again and he gives me two weeks. If I don't pay he'll hire a professional man to put a bullet in me. Now Driscoll was mostly bluff but

I took it serious. I had the police chief pull him in about his threat. Driscoll claimed he didn't remember doing any such thing, and if he did it were only a harmless joke during one of his drinking spells."

"You didn't think it was just a joke?"

"I dinna. I hired extra men to survey all new arrivals in town. Three or four more weeks go by and my mind's taken off Driscoll when my #2 mill burns down. But my men are still watching and that's when you come on the train from Chicago claiming to be a land speculator. We can't seem to pin down whether you're who you say you are and you act suspicious enough nosing around. Also, one of the clerks in the hotel reports a pistol among your things. Then you visit Driscoll's house and I'm next to certain you're the professional man he's hired, so I keep a close watch on your doings, as you know well enough. Each time you drew out your revolver at the bank we put a man on you, even if it was only the bank's janitor."

"You admit to employing Pattone and Shelvay then?"

"Can't say I know the names."

"Did you make any threats against Driscoll's life?"

"Don't recall any threats. Told him I weren't scared of him or anyone he might employ."

"Did Driscoll do anything further?"

"Some time later there was an arson attempted at my #1 mill. But my men sniffed it out and nipped it. I suspected Driscoll."

"Was that about the time Sam Washoo, Driscoll's man, was thrown into the streetcar?"

"Don't think so. Was the two gentlemen you mentioned earlier part of that?"

"They were."

"According to my reports drinking was involved."

Petronius said that was true.

"Dangerous business drinking," McClatchen observed.

"One thing puzzles me," said Petronius. "Why would a fella your size enjoy beating down a small man like Terence Driscoll?"

"It weren't for enjoyment."

"Then what?"

"You see, laddie, it ain't usually smart to get in a fight, but when you decide to fight you don't stop until the other man's down, and when's he down you put the boots to him. I learned that early, not just in the woods. I learned it during the war, riding with Phil Sheridan's army, burning and ripping through the Shennadoah Valley. That's what won the war and it's been my way of doing things since."

Petronius had the feeling McClatchen would offer him a job if he said the right words. But he didn't intend to say those words. He went on to his second request. "I would ask you to pay the balance of the money originally owed Terence Driscoll, to his daughter Addy Driscoll."

"Are ye now? You're here at her asking?"

"Entirely my own idea. She wouldn't seek favors from you. Likely she thinks you're a scoundrel and would say so to your face."

"And what do ye say to my face, laddie?"

Petronius hesitated for a second. "I say the same, though lots of folks think you're the sort of businessman the country needs to build prosperity. A year ago I had it in mind to be a man after yourself, hard and unyielding. Determined to put the boots to the other fella when I had him down. But now I'm dissuaded of that."

"What's dissuaded ye?" McClatchen challenged.

"Addy, and how she's conducted herself through all this."

McClatchen snorted. "Laddie, you ain't been dissuaded. You been turned you into a fool by a woman. You ain't the first."

"I'm fond of her, I admit."

"From what I know Addy Driscoll has grit and smartness.

I give her that. Got 'em from her mother not Terence Driscoll. You could do worse than her."

Petronius continued on. "Addy would like to keep her mill workers employed in some fashion. And she would work towards keeping Muskegon alive if she had the resources. This is a town you yourself have built, as much as anybody. Wouldn't you like to see it live on?"

McClatchen brushed aside the idea with a wave of his hand. "If the town goes on, fine. If she fades it won't bother me any. I'm not a man who needs to see his name on buildings and towns."

McClatchen got up and walked to a pile of account books and began to sort through them. "This might be the most uncongenial proposal ever put to me, laddie. To be asked for a cash gift while being tarred as a scoundrel." Yet he seemed more amused than offended as he leafed through a ledger.

"Not a gift. Money once honestly owed."

"It was, I admit. But you see I'll have need of all my cash in Washington State. I mean to log timber along Pudget Sound. That'll take investment, and I'll be bucking some big lumbermen."

Petronius could think of nothing to argue back. McClatchen went on. "Here's what I will do. I still own considerable property here in Muskegon. Real estate values are down now, because of the fire, so the whole of it might not be worth what was owed to Driscoll."

"Are you saying you'll give all your Muskegon property to Addy?"

"That's what I'm saying. I'll be all the quicker out to Washington State, and with my thoughts only for what's ahead. I'll have my lawyer make up a paper tomorrow morning. Is there any other request you have of me, laddie?"

Petronius had no other requests.

FINALE

Ryerson, Hills and Company, as a finale to its lumber business, has cut all the timber in the vicinity of its sawmill at the Bay Mills area of North Muskegon.

THOUSAND YEARS SUPPLY

Puget Sound has 1300 miles of shore line, and all along this line is one vast and unbroken forest of enormous trees. An official estimate places the amount of standing timber in that area at more than 500 billion feet, or a thousand years supply, even at the enormous rate the timber is being felled and sawed.

Muskegon Daily Chronicle

Ch 25

The next morning a messenger handed Petronius a large envelope which had the look and heft of legal documents. It was to be delivered to Addy, who was staying at Sam's farm east of town. Petronius immediately rented a carriage and drove out.

He found her in the field planting potatoes along with Sam and Joshua's mother.

"I'm glad you've come because we have something urgent to discuss." she said. "Shall we go back to the house?"

As they walked towards the small dwelling he said, "I've brought some rather interesting business myself." He handed her the envelope.

"What is it?"

"It's from McClatchen. The amount originally owed your father but in property rather than cash."

When they were seated at the kitchen table she opened the envelope and looked through the papers and documents in some puzzlement. There's a great deal of property here, especially in the south part of town. Why did McClatchen do this? What did you say to him?"

"I didn't threaten him at all. I went mainly to find out what went on between him and your father. He told me in some detail. I was surprised he even agreed to see me, but somehow he had me figured as a first class detective. Later I suggested he pay the rest of your father's claim. I don't think I was all that persuasive."

"Then why?"

"He said it was to speed his way out of town and get to Washington State all the quicker."

"I can't believe that." She shook her head in continued bewilderment

"If you'll forgive me for saying, it's more likely his joke on the city. A young woman, not too esteemed in the eyes of most folks here, suddenly made the city's largest property owner. That might be his idea of a good prank."

She laughed quietly. "That sounds closer to the truth."

"Or he may have felt some real debt of honor towards you. I didn't do a thorough job of questioning him on his motives and I can't say I begin to understand him. I do know he won't be told how to act by anyone else."

"I don't know what to think. I had just settled myself into accepting the simple life of a school teacher and now this. Yet I don't find it at all unwelcome." As she stuffed the papers back into the envelope Joshua came into the house and passed them without a word."

Addy suggested they go outside to talk further. They walked straight out into the field back of the house. Dozens of pine stumps had been dug out to make a clearing of several acres. The tangles of roots were lined along the edge of the field to form a rough fence.

"It's about Joshua. Sam came to me and said Joshua had taken his flint lock igniter and may have had something to do with the fire. The both of us talked with Joshua and he claims he started the fire. Do you believe that?"

Petronius felt a jolt. "I don't know what started the fire. It could have been an overturned oil lamp, or someone smoking in a barn."

"But Joshua is saying, and almost bragging, he did it."

Petronius wasn't able to put a lot of certainty in his voice. "I doubt he started the fire. Seems someone would have seen him. Of course, he puts himself in considerable danger claiming he did. There's men angry enough about their losses in the fire." He hesitated a bit before asking, "Did I influence Joshua with my talk of retribution do you think?"

"No more I expect than I influenced him in the opposite direction. He makes up his own mind now. He sees the life he enjoys, hunting and fishing, being taken away, and that makes him angry. And naturally he's infuriated when white people treat the Indians as an inferior race, almost obliged to die out."

"He and his family should leave before there's trouble. Is it just Sam and Joshua's mother here?"

"Yes, his father went off west somewhere years ago. He didn't like farming either. Joshua has always resented his father not taking him along, although he was only a baby at the time."

"Could they join his father now?"

"No one knows where he went."

"Then what do you suggest?"

"Perhaps a farm in a different state. One with some better land. This is just sand here, not fit for growing anything but trees."

"Wouldn't be a quick thing to do. And would Joshua be happy on another farm, even one with better soil?"

She admitted those were difficulties and they walked on in silence for a time. Then she said, "I think we have to find out whether Joshua did set the fire."

"How?"

Sawdust Fires 179

"We could take Joshua to the place and see if his claims make sense."

"I've been to the spot and there's nothing to be found."

She shook her head. "I don't know what else to propose."

They agreed to try the idea. But before they gathered up Joshua for the trip to town Addy had another thought. "Let's first go to where the Stimsons are staying and see Penelope. Joshua and Penelope have played together and they like each other."

"You're thinking Joshua will feel some remorse if he sees one of his casualties?"

"I don't know. But I can't believe Joshua would deliberately hurt people."

They rode to town in silence the whole way, Joshua not volunteering anything and Petronius holding off on questions.

If Addy was hoping the burned Stimson girl would look pitiful enough to bring some strong emotion from Joshua, then her hopes went unrealized. Penelope looked remarkably healthy. Her legs and the back of her dress bulged with bandages and dressings but she stretched easily on her side atop a small sofa and looked quite contented. She had been drawing pictures in a sketch book. She talked brightly and seemed happy enough to see Joshua and thanked him for visiting her. The boy returned her thanks with a stone-faced nod.

When they were in the carriage again Addy faced the boy. "Tell me now, Joshua. What is the truth? It's most important we know."

Joshua looked away and said, "My grandfather is angry with me. He said starting a fire is not a brave thing." Petronius was about to second the motion but Joshua went on. "The fire was already burning. I wanted the whole town to burn and I tried setting another building afire with the flint lock but I couldn't get it to work in the wind. I didn't start the fire but I wanted it to burn everything." He said nothing more.

Neither did the two adults, though they exchanged looks which were a mixture of relief and alarm.

Before they arrived back at the Washoo farm Addy asked, "Joshua, would you be happy if you could live with your father?"

"Nobody knows where he is."

"Yes, but if we could find him?"

"I would live with him."

"I'll talk to Sam and your mother and we'll see what can be done. Mind you, nothing is for certain."

Joshua stuck out his lower lip and his eyes took on an intense expression, as if he were concentrating very hard.

As soon as they arrived back at the farm Joshua jumped out of the carriage with the statement he was going into the house to pack.

"Not so quickly," Addy called after him. "Even if it's agreed, you won't be leaving this minute." She looked at Petronius and took a deep breath. "The truth isn't as bad as we thought."

"Not all that comforting either. The boy should get away somewheres, that's for certain."

She nodded and headed for the house. Petronius took the tired horse to a small shed for hay and water.

After another half hour Addy emerged. "His mother isn't willing to go and Sam's not keen on the idea either at his age. But he says he'll take Joshua west if you'll agree to go. He claims he needs someone with your youth, and," she had to smile, "your detective skills."

"My reputation as a first class detective grows."

They sat in the wagon seat to continue their talk.

"Would you be willing to go?" she asked.

"It could take months."

"I know, and we have no idea what the father's situation is or whether he'll accept Joshua. That's assuming you find the man."

Sawdust Fires 181

"Such an adventure does have an appeal for me. You have no intention of going yourself? Joshua would trust you more than me."

"He trusts his grandfather. And there's too much for me to do here in the months ahead." She again took the papers out of the legal envelope. "Look here! Besides the deeds McClatchen has put in plans for some new factories, including one to make ice boxes and another for washing machines. These should be tried. They'll use hardwood lumber, of which we still have plenty, and furnish employment as more mills close down."

"He may have had some feeling for saving the town at that. Do you mean to get involved in running those businesses yourself?"

"No. I'll hand that over to others. In fact I hope to dispose of all this property in the months ahead, but in some way which will benefit the city. Perhaps I can set up a fund of some type. I'll need to give the idea further thought."

He changed the subject. "Do you know anything about Willard Branson and a lumbering accident in Wisconsin?" He briefly described the incident.

"That explains some Wisconsin letters in my father's safe," she said. "But apparently he got nowhere with his inquiries. Either the man's death was an accident as McClathen claimed or else no one was willing to say different."

"Do you want to hear the rest of the details of what went on between your father and McClatchen?"

She sighed. "That can wait. We have so much else to think about."

"That's true. So what of the school teaching work now?"

"I haven't changed on that. I'm determined to lead a simpler life. I'll stay with Joshua's mother and help her with the farming. She's already invited me."

"We'll that's neat enough. Now what about us, you and

I?"

"I've thought over what you said to me earlier. Have you also?"

"I have and I'm not ready to take any of it back."

She took his hand. "Then I accept your proposal if that's what it was."

"It was a proposal. And your acceptance brings me joy."

They rode for some time in quiet, holding hands.

"I have an odd question," she said. "Was your feeling of joy just now as intense as your dream about the baseball pavilion?"

He thought for a moment. "No, it wasn't. I have to be truthful. Of course that was a only a dream."

"I believe it was real, just as real as my feelings atop the pine tree." She furrowed her brow in deep thought for a few moments."

"Are you coming back to town with me," he interrupted, "for some sort of celebration?"

She agreed and they headed west again. The horse was let walk at its slowest pace.

"I don't have an engagement present for you," he said. "My wealth now amounts to about six dollars and 80 cents, and a lot of that will go to the livery stable."

"I know a gift I'd like. Would you return to the name of Peter? I don't think I could marry a Petronius, or even a Angus."

"That gift is within my budget."

"I'd like to make dinner for us as my engagement gift to you, but my cooking skills are childish as yet. And I don't have money either for a restaurant."

"Perhaps Mrs. Charlton will accept a guest at her table if she knows it's to be an engagement supper. The schedule calls for stew I believe."

"Kind Mrs. Charlton."

"What's next on our agenda?"

"Tomorrow morning we should arrange an appointment with Father Van Grough. The marriage banns will have to be announced. Then we'll need to raise cash for your trip west. What do you think? Is there a chance of finding Joshua's father?"

"Seems unlikely if you look at the size of those western territories. But maybe the man left some clues with his family about what he intended and where he'd try it. I thought too of writing my friend Jacob Larson in Arizona. Maybe he'd help. In any case I'll send back reports."

"I won't know where to write but I'll send my prayers," she said.

"I'd like a picture of you to take with me."

"I haven't any recent pictures. For years I've resisted being photographed. All I have is those sketches I did of myself."

"I'll take one."

"And I'll have the sketch I made of you." She brushed away a tear with her free hand. "As you said yesterday we're damaged goods. But I believe we'll make a pair," she couldn't help laughing through her tears as she searched for the right words, "as interesting as any."

"Done well at it so far."

"Have you given any thought as to what you'll do after you come back?"

"If my fame as a first class detective hasn't dimmed by then, I'll easily get a job with the local police force. I'll try to do little harm until such time as the force sponsors a baseball team. Then I'll offer my services as coach."

She smiled. "I'm convinced you'll do fine, if you follow your best instincts."

Peter kissed her on her scarred cheek, and then kissed her on her slightly scarred but still desirable lips.

WISH

Women wish to be loved without a why or a wherefore, not because they are pretty, or good, or well bred, or graceful, or intelligent, but because they are themselves.

Muskegon Daily Chronicle

THE END

Sawdust Fires 185

CHAPTER HEADINGS AND EXCERPTS

Ch 1 - LUMBER QUEEN: from the book *Muskegon and Its Resources*, found in the Muskegon room of Hackley Library

Ch 2 - PROMISING OUTLOOK: from the 1889-90 City Directory, found in the Muskegon room of Hackley Library

Ch 3 - TERRIBLE LOSS: Muskegon Daily Chronicle (MDC) Sep 9, 1890

Ch 4 - DON'TS FOR GOOD GIRLS: MDC, Jan 18, 1889

Ch 5 - EVOLUTION EXPLAINED: MDC, Jan 20, 1889

Ch 6 - UNUSUALLY FREE: MDC, Jan 9, 1891

Ch 7 - RIGHT TRACK: MDC, Jan 9, 1891

Ch 8 - SHORTCOMINGS: MDC, Feb 4, 1891

Ch 9 - MANGLED: MDC, Jul 7, 1888

Ch 10 - TREND: MDC, Sep 27, 1890

Ch 11 - FAST: motto mentioned in several histories

Ch 12 - SO MANY: MDC, Jan 3, 1891

Ch 13 - LIE TO CHILDREN: MDC, Jul 2, 1889

Ch 14 - HIGHER PLANE: MDC, Jul 2, 1889

Ch 15 - DISTANT DAYS: MDC, Nov 20, 1890

Ch 16 - SOCIAL SUCCESS: MDC, Feb 9, 1889

Ch 17 - NO QUIETUDE: MDC, Dec 17, 1890

Ch 18 - CULTIVATED TASTE: MDC, Jan 18, 1889

Ch 19 - PERFECT YOUTH: MDC, Jul 11, 1889

Ch 20 - SORROW: MDC, Jan 15, 1889

Ch 21 - WATER PROBLEM: MDC, Jul 2, 1889

Ch 22 - IN RUINS: MDC, May 18, 1891

Ch 23 - SNUB: MDC, May 18, 1891

Ch 24 - REBUILD: MDC, May 18, 1891

Ch 25 - FINALE: MDC, Jan 17, 1891
      THOUSAND YEARS SUPPLY: MDC, Jul 12, 1889
      WISH: MDC, Jul 12, 1889